APACHE SHADOWS

Albert R. Booky

Sunstone Press
Santa Fe, New Mexico

Dedicated to my granddaughter, Audra Lee

First Edition

Printed in the United States of America

Library of Congress Cataloging in Publication Data:

Booky, Albert R., 1925-
    Apache shadows.

    1. Apache Indians--Fiction. 2. Indians of North
America--Fiction. I. Title.
PS3552.06436A83   1986   813'.54   85-30435
ISBN: 0-86534-084-6

Published in 1986 by SUNSTONE PRESS
                Post Office Box 2321
                Santa Fe, NM 87504-2321 / USA

FOREWORD

Since the beginning of time, the blending of cultures has produced change. The mingling and melting of two or more societies into a new and sometimes more dynamic force often results in a better society.

It was Alexander the Great's conquest of the then known world which placed in motion, on a large scale, the blending of the Greek civilization with that of the East. This blending produced new societies, each with its own unique culture and life style.

The Roman Empire continued the pattern established by Alexander and because of the assimilation of other nationalities and peoples into the Roman Empire, its tenure of life was perhaps extended for hundreds of years.

The melting of Spanish blood with that of the American Indian produced the mestizo. The French and English have also mingled, blended and have made their contribution to this process.

Alexander dreamed of a world in which people could live together in harmony and security, free from the fear of attack by another.

This book is an attempt to focus attention upon the Apache culture and customs and recognize that they can contribute much in making our society into a more energetic, vibrant, and enduring entity.

All Americans must learn to accept and appreciate the qualities of all of our peoples. It is vital that we nurture our unique heritage or destroy ourselves from within. The choice is ours to make. Only time will tell if we have chosen the right path.

CHAPTER ONE

*"I believe the Indian to be in body
and mind equal to the white man."*
Thomas Jefferson: Letter to
F.J. Chastellux, 1785

T he day was exceptionally clear and sunny, and a warm breeze
wafted through the tops of the tall Ponderosa pines. An
Apache woman and her two children gathered wild berries at the
foot of the Sierra Blanca Mountains, those mountains sacred to the
Mescalero Apaches in southcentral New Mexico Territory.

Her son stopped picking and stared long at the snow-covered
peaks towering over them. His sister glanced in his direction and
began to tease him about looking for excuses to get out of women's
work, but seeing his troubled expression, she walked toward him,
her low laughter ceasing as she tugged at his arm and asked, "Is
there something wrong, my brother?"

He did not hear her at first, so intently did he gaze, and she
tugged again at his arm, repeating her question. A short distance
away, their mother rose from her stooped position and with a few
berries still in her hand, she joined them inquiringly. She heard her
son say, "I feel something strange here," he pressed his chest and
continued, "I don't feel sick, but I guess you could call it a pain,
though not a physical pain."

"Explain yourself," his mother told him.

"Is he all right, mother?" The young maiden looked inquiringly at her mother with a troubled face.

"Let your brother speak," her mother commanded. "Continue, my son."

"Our Apache God, Usen, lives on that mountain and he talks
to the Apache warriors who ask for his guidance and help. I want to
go to Him for something in me tells me to go, but an equally strong
feeling resists, telling me not to seek Him. What does that mean,
mother? You are older and wiser than me; tell me why these two
feelings are clashing within my heart."

Their mother's eyes filled with tears as she sought for a way to
express her misgivings. Her lips parted and she tried to speak and
still no words came. She buried her face in her hands as her two
children looked at one another and then back at their mother. She
uttered no sound, but tears wet her hands, and she fell to her knees
and murmured something inaudible to her listeners. Quickly the

children knelt by their mother, one on either side of her. The girl hugged her, trying to find words of comfort, though why they were needed she did not know. Her son put his hand on her shoulder, patting it, and asked, "Mother, did I say something wrong? Did I offend you?"

Their mother looked at each of them in turn as she wiped the tears from her face. "Sit down," she said in her accustomed calm manner. "There is something I must tell you."

When they were seated near her she began, "I am not an Apache, and so you are only half Apache. As you know, your father is a Mescalero Apache, but what you didn't know is that he captured me when I was a young girl and made me his wife. We have you both and of course your older brother who is at this very minute on a raid with your father. That is why you have feelings which seem to conflict, my son. One is the white man's feeling and the other is that of the Apache. Remember, you have known no other way of life, and that gives you stronger Apache feelings, perhaps, than those of the white man."

Her two children looked at one another in shock and were silent, each pondering this strange new idea, until her daughter spoke in a soft, compassionate voice, "We are part white eyes?"

Her mother placed an arm around each of her children as she nodded.

The boy's back straightened as he asked, "How old were you when you were captured, mother?"

"Let me tell you the story, at least as much as I can remember. Many moons from here, in the direction of where the sun awakes, is a place where the white man's chief lives . . . it is called Washington."

"Wash-shing-tone?"

"No, my son, your words are not correct. It is not Wash-shing-tone. Do not separate the word into three parts, for it is only one word. Listen closely if you wish to learn how to say the white man's word, Washington.

"It would take many, many days of riding to reach there on horseback from here. There you would see that the white eyes' tribes are as many as the trees of the forest or the grasses of the Llano Estacado. Far too many for even the mighty Apache nation to destroy. Some day, the Apaches and their way of life may be no more. The white eyes live in villages of all sizes, and some of these villages have as many people in them as in all of our Apache villages put together. They have the problems which so many people living close together can cause. Some of them drink brown water which makes them crazy, and they try to corrupt our people with this firewater and our people do not realize the danger and heartbreak which the firewater can bring.

"They have tepees with iron walls to keep their lawbreakers locked up when they break their tribal laws. They will destroy Usen's land in every way we could imagine as their villages grow ever larger. With this growth, comes change which is against the way of Usen. Families will break apart, losing their love for one another. All this is what my mother and father wished to leave behind when they left the place of the rising sun.

"My father worked for the chief of the white eyes in Washington and he and my mother were being sent to do the work of the chief in El Paso del Norte. On their way there, my mother became sick and died, but my father continued on, and after he and the others of our party had left the Mexican village of Las Vegas, the wagon train was attacked by Comanches, and my father and many others were killed. During this attack, a war party of Apaches was nearby, and being Apaches, the superior people, they were quick to take advantage of the attack by helping to drive the Comanches away. The white men did not know the ways of the Apaches, so the cunning of the war party paid big dividends. They pretended to be friends of the white men and after all, hadn't they proved their friendship by saving them from the Comanches? The white men rewarded them with many gifts, but no weapons were bestowed upon the disappointed Apaches. That night in retaliation, the Apaches stole many guns and some children. I was one of those children who was stolen away as the white men slept. You asked how old I was when the Apaches stole me? I was fourteen years old."

"Mother, you must also have two different feelings in your chest if you were not born Apache. Is this not true?"

"Yes, my son, I do."

"Did you ever try to escape and return to your people, mother?" Her daughter moved closer to show her sympathy for her mother's dilemma.

"No, because I became pregnant soon afterward and after your oldest brother was born, I knew that I must stay with my family." She touched her daughter gently on the arm and continued, "Some day, my daughter, you will understand my feelings. Later, both of you came along and I had no desire to return, and no choice, really, but to become an Apache in spirit as well as in reality. You see, if I had gone back to my people, they would have scorned me for having been married to an Apache brave and for having borne his children. I would have been an outcast among my own people. I would probably have been called a squaw, a degrading word in their language. My concern was not for myself, but for the three of you, and will continue to be. What will become of you as the white men or white eyes as our people call them, become more and more numerous, as they surely will? What does the future hold for the Apache? I'm afraid that our future is not very bright."

"Mother, why do you call us Apaches and father refers to our people as Shis Inday?"

"Your father is correct in referring to us as the Shis Inday for the name means 'Men of the Woods'. I suppose I still use the term, 'Apache' because that is what other people call us, whether it be American, Mexican, or other Indian tribes, and I might add, many of our own people also use this term. We are also referred to as 'The People' or 'Dine' or just plain 'Inde'."

"What does Apache mean, mother?" her daughter questioned.

"Enemy," her mother answered proudly.

"Enemy to whom?" came the next question.

"To all who enter our country to do us harm, or enter our country without our permission."

"Father calls you Evening Star. Why?"

"Because that is the time of day that he took me from the wagon train," their mother replied as she rose. "We must be getting back to the village to welcome your father and brother when they return, which should be soon."

She paused and went on, "And remember, children, I have come to love your father deeply, as he does me, and to love this life as the Apache lives it."

The faces of the children mirrored the quiet happiness of their mother as the three walked toward the village.

"I'll be proud when I can go with father and Crazy Legs on raids and bring back fine things for the two of you," the boy said. "After four such raids, I will be given a name, a name that only I will own, as Crazy Legs does his name."

"Your father told me that he will take you on your first raid next year if you are ready," she smiled.

"Mother, tell us again how Crazy Legs got his name," said her daughter.

"Well, when he went out on his second raid, which was into Sonora, Mexico, your father was with them. The raiding party was looking around the country for a good target when they heard about a Mexican soldier by the name of Lieutenant Morales who was then in the town of Cananea. Our warriors had heard a rumor from some peons that two days before that the lieutenant and his men had captured an Apache warrior. It was said that the lieutenant had taken his captive into the little town with a lot of fanfare. The Apache was riding his pony, but had his hands tied behind his back. The lieutenant yelled to the townspeople to come out of their houses to see the large gopher which they'd captured. As they rode, the lieutenant repeatedly slashed the warrior across the face with his pistol, until his face dripped with blood. His nose was broken and he had many cuts on his head and face which bled freely, but he rode his pony as an Apache should under such circumstances, sitting his horse as if he were a conquering hero, never uttering a cry or murmur because of the pain which he suffered.

"This infuriated the Mexican lieutenant who was determined to make the Apache humble himself in some way. He ordered one of his men to bring a rope which he fastened around the waist of the Apache and then had him hung from a tree. The soldiers left him hanging there while they repaired to a nearby cantina to buy some courage in the form of tequila for what they intended to do to the Apache later.

"This is when your brother rode into Cananea dressed as a Mexican peon. He was not noticed for there were many more peons in the little village. Your brother's assignment was to draw a lot of attention to himself to give your father and the others time to rescue the Apache and get him well away. Your brother dismounted and entered the cantina where the soldiers were drinking, and as he passed through the door, his legs wobbled as if they were made of rubber and his speech was not much better, as though he had been drinking to excess. By this time, the lieutenant and his men had a good start of their own and delighted in the sight which your brother made. Your brother must have put on a good show, indeed, for he was asked to join them, which he did. When he judged it was time, he left by the rear door, but not before he had baited the lieutenant, asking, 'What do you plan to do to that Apache, General?'"

"The lieutenant appreciated being addressed as a general and your brother attempted to come to attention to salute the lieutenant, but failed miserably, thus provoking another round of laughter. But when he had reached the alley behind the cantina, his legs improved miraculously, no longer resembling two twisted juniper limbs. He slipped to the rear door of the bank next door and built a small fire on the steps and placed several bullets in the fire. He then hid in the shadows and when the bullets began to explode, he began throwing rocks through the windows of the bank and also the cantina, yelling, 'Bank robbery!'

"The drunken soldiers, as well as some of the people of the town ran out of the buildings nearby to try to catch the robbers. In the confusion, your brother threw his knife from the shadows, striking Lieutenant Morales in the center of the back. Your brother then rode to join the rest of the war party. The braves who rode with your father and brother laughed and began to call your brother Crazy Legs, because of his acting. During the remainder of their absence from our village they continued to joke with your brother about his acting, calling him Crazy Legs. It began as a joke, but later became accepted as his title.

"That's how your brother received his name, as is customary, from something they do." She looked at them proudly, "For that is the way of the Apache and a way which I have learned to accept and approve, for I consider myself a good Apache, and a good wife and mother."

"Mother," the boy said hesitantly, "do you think my father will be home today?"

"I don't know," Evening Star answered, "it depends upon many things; your father may have encountered problems which could delay him. Why do you ask?"

"If father might not be home today, I would like to climb the sacred mountain and ask Usen some questions. Would that be all right?"

"Yes, my son, but be careful."

"I will," the boy answered as he looked up at the snow-clad peaks of the Sierra Blancas and began to walk up the slope. "I will," they heard him mutter to himself as he walked.

"Will he be all right?" His sister, Blue Bird, looked questioningly at her mother and then back at the thick forest where her brother had vanished from sight.

"Yes, my child, he'll be all right. Usen will see to that. He has reached the time in his life which tugs at the Apache in him. He wants answers to many questions which trouble him and only he can find the answers. Let's leave him for he'll come home when he's ready."

The boy climbed steadily upward for hours until he had reached the elevation where the Aspen trees abounded. The white-barked trees at first mingled with the huge Ponderosa pines, but as he had continued ever upward, the pines became fewer until at last he stood in the midst of beautiful aspens. He stood drinking in the beauty which surrounded him on all sides, then looked back in the direction from which he had come. Mile after mile of the pines extended below him in the stark moonlight. They covered the rolling hills and hidden valleys. He then turned to look upwards once again and could see the timberline below the upper slopes of the snow-covered ground.

"Usen?" He spoke in a soft and gentle murmur, "Are you there, Usen?" He fell to his knees and gazed at the snow-covered peak above him, at the highest point in the Sierra Blanca mountain range.

"I have come to speak with you," he said as his eyes searched the snowy slopes.

"Usen . . . Usen . . . Usen . . . Usen," he repeated it four times, in a barely audible tone, four times, for that is the sacred number to most Indians, and it was also true for the Apaches. He then began a chant which the medicine man had taught to him over a period of many months. The chant continued for many moments and then he was silent for an equal length of time, after which he spoke once more, "Usen, I seek part of your power. I humble myself before you in complete subjugation to your will, to your spirit, to your power. I ask that you release a portion of your power to me, one of your devoted creations. I will use that power only to glorify your being."

How long he knelt there among the aspens he did not know, but snow had begun to fall as he continued his chanting, then another period of silence, then another attempt to converse with his god. His hair became covered with the soft, pure white snow, his shoulders concealed by it as well as most of the lower part of his legs as they extended out behind him.

Nightfall once more crept over the mountain as the lone figure continued its vigil. Animals of all kinds heard his voice as they passed in the distance. They were puzzled and frightened at the strange sight and did not hesitate long enough to investigate. The night shadows passed over the mountain until all was dark, even the trees around the boy obscured, then in the dark stillness a bright half moon slowly came into sight as it slipped from behind the tree-clad slopes and continued its journey across the sky. Stars began to twinkle down upon the lone figure as the boy continued his prayerful chant and then observed moments of silence. A feeling then came to the boy, a feeling of peace, of solitude, a feeling of complete safety, a feeling of warmth, a warmth which he had never experienced before in his entire young life, until this moment.

His bowed head slowly lifted toward the sky as he opened his eyes, his hands still clasped before his chest. A voice could be heard within him as he fixed his eyes upon a single star which seemed to twinkle at him alone. The voice said, "Man is evil and man is good. Man is faced with evil and man is faced with good. I now bring light to your soul, a light which has come from O'zho. This light can replace darkness wherever it is found. A light that can destroy evil and glorify good. I want you to bring this light into all people's hearts. When this light enters the soul of man, he will know me and be as me. We will be as one." The voice ceased and the eyes of the boy were still fixed on that one twinkling star. A cloud now passed between the boy and the star, and as the cloud moved on, the star was not to be seen. The boy looked frantically for his star, to no avail. He finally stood, staggering from his long vigil, and brushed the snow from his head and shoulders. It was knee deep now as he searched for stones with his feet. He must have rocks with which to build an altar on the spot where he had knelt. When he had finished placing the stones, he broke limbs from the underbrush, placing them among the rocks. When this had been done, he stepped back and inspected his work. He decided that the altar needed something distinctive to set it aside from other rocks nearby and so he removed his headband and entangled it in one of the limbs which protruded from the stone altar. I will make another headband when I return to my village, only my new one will have my twinkling star on it, the boy told himself. Before he left the place, he knelt once more and chanted four more times. This done, he began his descent down the snowy mountainside. How long he had been on the mountain, he didn't know.

His father and brother had returned triumphantly with the other warriors who had made up the party and the victory celebration was over.

"It has been nearly two days since we saw you walk into the forest," Evening Star told him as she welcomed her son. "When you have eaten and rested, you may tell us about your pilgrimage."

When the boy's story was told, it spread like wildfire through the camp, and the people gathered to ask questions. Among them was a diyin or medicine man. He had in days' past proven to his band that he was a dreamer of dreams as well as interpreter of visions. He was a respected and honored interpreter of events such as the boy had experienced.

"A great star has chosen to favor you, son of Thunderbolt and Evening Star. This star is one of the messengers of Usen. Listen to this message and do its bidding, Sons-in-jah (Great Star), for this will be your name, to be used only by you and no other, and once you have performed the requirements proscribed by the laws of our people, you will take your place among our warriors. Then, and only then, will your name be officially known among our warriors. If someone else wishes to give this name to their newly born son or daughter (Apache names do not denote gender), they must first get your permission. This name must not be used loosely, but only on fitting occasions, for it has been presented to you by Usen. He has spoken. I have spoken." The diyin turned and walked away and was followed by the others.

Thunderbolt turned to his son proudly and placed his hands on the boy's shoulders saying, "Sons-in-jah . . . that is a good name. We will have to hasten your training so that you may accompany me on four raiding parties. Then your name will be official."

During the cold, winter months, Thunderbolt found that his son was a fast learner with an excellent memory. He was pleased, for he told his son, "Remembering is one of the most important disciplines of a new young mind. Give your strongest efforts to this aspect of your training, for without a good memory, messages can be wrongly reported to another, which in turn could cause much hardship or even death. It is important that you train your memory for all of the reasons which I have just mentioned, in addition to many others which you yourself have the intelligence to understand. If we have poor memories, who is to tell our history to those who come after us? We do not make lines on paper as the white eyes do to keep their history. We keep our history locked up in the safest place which Usen has given us," he said as he touched his forehead with a finger.

Thunderbolt instructed his son in how to use the terrain to become part of the landscape. "Wet a blanket and rub in dirt, clay, vegetation, even walnut juice to make the blanket appear as a rock, ground, or whatever you wish it to resemble," he told him.

The lessons continued throughout the winter months; sometimes the two of them went out into the field to learn firsthand.

When spring arrived, Sons-in-jah was ready for his first raid, one year sooner than his father had expected.

"Now, remember, you have to do all of the chores for the older warriors when they ask you and also whatever else you think should be done without being asked. The last is particularly important because if you fail in this you are not ready to be admitted as a warrior when the council holds its meetings for this purpose. Four such raids of doing your duty as required by our laws are necessary before you become a full-fledged warrior."

To his father's great pride, Great Star went on his four raids and was voted by the council to be accepted by them as a warrior without one dissenting vote.

CHAPTER TWO

E ight Apache warriors rode in single file as they followed Crazy Legs down the western slopes of the Sierra Blancas. Not a word was spoken until the raiding party had reached a bend in the Tularosa River, not far from the base of the mountain.

Crazy Legs paused at the edge of the high river bank at the bottom of which flowed the small stream of water. Its appearance was deceiving, for although it was usually content to wander placidly through the high cuts, it sometimes earned the right to be designated a river, for during flash flooding or the spring run-off from the melting of the winter's snows, it could rampage right over its banks, creating havoc as it ran.

Crazy Legs could look out over the open prairie and see the white sands shimmering in the bright sunlight. When the warriors were assembled, he spoke, "We will cross the prairie until we reach the white sands where we'll find it easy to conceal ourselves among the dunes. Our journey will then take us south until we leave the white sands and enter upon the desert home of the yucca, mesquite, and tall grass which cover the next forty miles of our journey. If we should be attacked by Mexicans or Americans, we shall split up, going in nine different directions, and rendezvous at our base in the San Andres Mountains or back here in the Sierra Blanca stronghold, or if neither of these places can be reached, hide in the Sacramento Mountains; you know where.

"I will lead our column and my brother will bring up the rear. Remember, no talking or making of any sounds which will reveal our location. If there are no questions, follow me."

They rode at a steady trot, slowly enough to preserve the strength of their ponies. Expert horsemen have always thus sought to save their mounts, for upon that reserve depends the safety of their riders.

When the raiding party reached the southern end of the San Andres Mountain range near the San Augustin Pass, Crazy Legs talked more of what he hoped to accomplish. "El Paso del Norte lies to our south, less than half a day's ride. We'll camp here and start early in the morning. Once there, we'll skirt the village on its west side. If we find no rewards there, we'll head for Casas Grandes, not far from the Sierra Madre Mountains of Mexico. There we will hope to be able to gather some horses or whatever else is available without any losses to ourselves."

Perhaps twenty miles northwest of Casas Grandes, in the

foothills of the Sierra Madres, the Mescaleros rested their horse on top of a high, steep cliff. All nine of them sat in a row, with Crazy Legs in the middle. They were watching three horsemen on the plain below as they urged their mounts to their fastest possible speed. In the distance behind them and making a large dust cloud followed a band of horsemen. To judge by the amount of dust being stirred up, there were many more riders in the second bunch.

Crazy Legs untied the pouch from his saddle and took out a pair of binoculars. Shortly the others heard him mutter, "Apaches, being pursued by Mexican soldiers. Quickly! Prepare a smoke signal."

The Apaches gathered green juniper, pinon, and cedar limbs, piling them at the edge of the cliff.

"We have time for only one signal," Crazy Legs told them. "I hope our brothers see it."

With a blanket, the Mescaleros kept the smoke boxed in until there was enough accumulated to make a good signal. The green boughs worked well, and Crazy Legs barked, "Now!" A smoke signal rose instantly into the windless sky.

"Now mount your ponies and we'll go to the aid of our brothers."

The three Apaches on the floor of the desert far below had seen the smoke, but gave no hint of having seen it. They were hoping that the soldiers had missed the significance of it, if in fact they had seen it.

Crazy Legs and his braves descended the mountain and reached the level ground behind the soldiers. The three Apaches had gained the shelter of huge boulders at the foot of the mountainside and were dismounted and firing back at the soldiers. Several of the soldiers had fallen before their comrades realized that not all of the firepower was coming from the rocks. This availed them not at all, however, for the deadly cross fire soon wiped out the remainder of the troops.

"Why were the Mexican soldiers chasing you?" Crazy Legs asked the three Apaches while his men inspected the dead soldiers.

"We were trying to free our women from the Mexicans. They have my wife and two daughters, and the two braves who ride with me have also lost women. We lost one brave who was killed by the soldiers not far from Casas Grandes. You know as well as I do that once the women are taken from the village to the mines, it will be almost impossible to rescue them."

Crazy Legs looked around at the bodies of the soldiers. "Take their uniforms, we'll need them more than they will. We're going to help our Chiricahua brothers to free their women."

The Chiricahua warriors looked at one another, but displayed no emotion, and their spokesman asked matter of factly, "What is your plan?"

"Bring the uniform of the Mexican leader here," Crazy Legs ordered. Within a few minutes he had donned the uniform of the Mexican officer and the others began to get an inkling of what he was planning.

"With those clothes you look as much like a Mexican as you do an Apache," one of the Chiricahuas told him.

"The reason I do not look like an Apache, my friend, is because I am half white eyes. I also speak the white eyes' tongue and the Mexican tongue as if I were one of them."

"Tell us your plan, my brother," Great Star said.

"I will write an order telling the Mexicans in Casas Grandes to release the women to me. The order will come from Mexico City and will bear the name of the chief of all the Mexican soliers, Antonio Juan Mendoza. Search the saddle bags of the Mexican leader; it should have order papers. They always have such papers because the Mexican soldier does not do anything without such orders!"

"But you cannot go alone, my brother, and besides they will not think the government in Mexico City would be stupid enough to send one soldier to bring back all of the women. They would suspect you."

"My brother," Crazy Legs grinned, "you will be a great warrior someday, for you show great promise in your thinking. We, you and I, will never become chiefs, but we will be great warriors; too bad that only a fullblooded Apache may become a chief, but because of your deeds we will be spoken well of around the campfires on cold winter nights." As he spoke, he laid an arm across the shoulder of his younger brother.

Then turning to the others, he said, "All of you put on the uniforms of the soldiers and we will wait until the women are being shipped to the mines and then we will overtake them. My brother and I will approach the Mexican soldiers, for he, too, can be mistaken for a Mexican. The rest of you will remain at a distance until we call."

Thirty-one women prisoners were placed in wagons as the sun

began to peep over a distant mountain range. They wore iron bracelets around both wrists and ankles, with a chain extending between wrists and ankles. They shuffled from the adobe jail between two rows of Mexican soldiers who held rifles at the ready. Some of the townspeople watched with sober faces, and a few cried out the names of relatives, for not all of the women were Apaches. Three soldiers were on horseback, one of them giving orders to hurry them along. When all of the women were loaded, another officer came out of the jail. He was followed closely by the local militia captain. They shook hands and saluted one another. Now the soldiers began to move the wagons out, down the dusty street toward the desert.

The women were a pitiful sight, ragged, with unkempt hair, and far from clean. Their faces were devoid of hope; their eyes sunken deeply into their skulls, were those of the dead. They were seated six to a wagon with the extra one riding horseback. They were terribly crowded, for the wagons also carried provisions for the mines.

The fate of anyone unfortunate enough to be sent to the mines was known by all and some of the prettier ones had already had a sort of initiation course while being held in the jail. Because of this, the soldiers had been instructed to watch them carefully to prevent any chance of suicide among them, hence the shackles.

The dreadful scene was closely observed by one Mexican bystander who slipped away from the little knot of people who watched in pity, but afraid to intervene. Great Star, dressed as a peon, walked between two buildings and mounting his pony, walked it quietly out of town.

When he told what he had observed, his listeners were infuriated. "Mount up," Crazy Legs said as he sprang into his Mexican saddle. "We have work to do, very important work . . . remember to ride in twos as the soldiers do, and my brother and I will ride in the lead." He broke into a trot as they moved out to meet the wagons.

Ten miles out from Casas Grandes, Crazy Legs made his move. Because the wagons were slow moving, the Mexicans guarding them were forced to a slow pace also. Crazy Legs and Great Star rode up behind the wagons at a trot, leaving the others some distance behind. The Mexicans heard the approaching riders and halted the wagontrain. The commanding officer, a major, turned his horse and rode back to meet these new arrivals.

"Sir," Crazy Legs said when they had met and saluted the

major, "Sir, I have orders from General Mendoza in Mexico City to bring these prisoners to him."

"Why, what would he want with these poor specimens?"

"I don't know sir, all I know is that he ordered me to bring them back with me. Here are my orders, sir." Crazy Legs took the orders from his coat pocket.

The major scanned the orders and finally looked up frowning, "But I don't know a General Mendoza."

"Sir, he is from the state of Chiapas. He has been transferred to Mexico City."

"The son of some rich patron, no doubt," the major concluded, "who knows the presidente. The papers look in order," he said after a pause. "Very well, you may have the prisoners. Frankly, I am very pleased that I don't have to make that hot, dusty trip all the way to the mining camps."

While Crazy Legs was talking with the major, Great Star had ridden up along the wagon train pretending to inspect the prisoners. When he reached the head wagon, he dismounted and walked back along the five wagons. When he was certain that all of the women in the wagons were not Mexican, he whispered "Ish-tra-nay (women) Shis Inday Nejeunee (Wood people Apaches)." As he said this, he walked by each wagon. The women did not change expressions, but if one had looked closely into their eyes, he would have seen the beginning of twinkles of happiness and hope replacing their looks of despair.

The Mexicans turned back toward Casas Grandes and Crazy Legs motioned for the other Apaches to replace the Mexican guards along side the wagons. It was a happy sight to see the Mexican soldiers riding at a brisk trot toward Casas Grandes and Crazy Legs and his Apaches walking their horses in another direction. When at length, the soldiers had passed out of sight and hearing, the women cried aloud in their joy at being delivered and their deliverers joined in their happiness.

"There'll be none of that," Crazy Legs cautioned, though with a grin on his face, "we're not out of danger yet. When we've reached the Sierra Madres and safety, then we'll celebrate."

Twenty-four of the prisoners were Mexican women who sat in their places fearful of what would happen to them, expecting the Apaches to kill them or take them prisoner. Crazy Legs rode up to the wagons and spoke to them, asking, "Which one of you can speak for the others?"

No one spoke for a few seconds until Crazy Legs spoke again,

"I know one can be your spokesman. We've no time to waste, either your leader can be your spokesman, or we will do what we have to do."

Several of the women turned to one woman in particular, and Crazy Legs addressed her, "You, we could use your help, and I do not have time for woman talk, yes or no, what is your answer?"

The woman whose name was Magdalena searched the eyes of the women around her and replied in a low voice, "Yes, we will help." She realized that time was an important element so she asked for no conditions, hoping that if they trusted to the honor of the Apaches, they would not be disappointed, but she kept her eyes fixed on the Apache's, showing in her own way that she expected something in return.

"We will remember," Crazy Legs answered, in a tone which Magdalena accepted as her assurance of safety, and other conditions.

The Apache leader now spoke to his warriors. "Take off the Mexican soldiers' uniforms and put them into the wagons. We may need them later . . . and then remove the shackles from the women."

Turning back to his braves and Great Star, he told them, "Go with my brother to locate the horses of the dead soldiers and bring them back immediately. We'll need all of those horses, so don't fail. Now go!" The Apaches thus designated raced in the direction of the fifteen dead soldiers.

"Prepare the horses for a journey; a journey which should please you," Crazy Legs said as he turned his head and fixed his eyes on Magdalena. The Mexican woman saw in the eyes of the Apache what she had hoped for, revenge . . . revenge to those who had done her and the others so much wrong. A smile crossed her lips and she nodded and turned to the other women, saying, "You heard what he said, get those horses ready for a journey."

The Apache leader looked down from his horse at the woman and with his eyes expressed approval. She smiled at him and raised both hands, turned her head slightly to one side and with a half smile said, "What am I to do . . . I'm a born leader!"

The Apache sprang off his horse and said the the Mexican woman, "You know that we are going back to Casas Grandes, don't you?"

She nodded.

"When the women are finished with the horses, I want you to meet with them and find out whom they want punished back there in Casas Grandes for the injustice which they had inflicted upon them. We will not have time to correct all of the unjustice, keep that in mind, but we want . . ."

"I understand," Magdalena interrupted, "We will not delay or hinder your departure from here any longer than necessary. Maybe we will need less time than you and your braves will need to do what you have planned for Casas Grandes." The breeze blew a strand of hair across her face and with one hand she pushed it away. Her face grew stern and a look of hatred replaced her smile. "We will be quick and thorough and we'll never be forgotten in Casas Grandes, or for that matter anywhere else in Mexico."

Crazy Legs began to speak, but her attention was far away, and finally in exasperation he shouted, "Woman, come back to today, the yesterdays are behind you now!"

The Mexican woman shook her head and then looked up at Crazy Legs, saying, "I am listening now, so speak."

"Tell me about Casas Grandes, where the soldiers are, where they keep their horses, where they store their guns, what we can take from the village which will not slow our return to our people."

Magdalena and the Apache sat down in the shade of one of the wagons and discussed Casas Grandes, its defences, its weaknesses, as far as she knew, and came up with a plan of attack and retreat. When they had finished, he called the seven Apache women to him and instructed them to ride around Casas Grandes at such a distance that they would not be seen. "Scout the area thoroughly. You are Apaches, so you know what I want. We do not need or want unwelcome visitors to interrupt our visit to the village. You will know when we leave Casas Grandes. We will leave from the north end of town, so have one of your scouts stationed at a strategic location to watch when we leave and under what circumstances. She will inform the rest of you when it is time to join us. Take whatever weapons you need."

The Apache women said nothing as they each took up a rifle, and sufficient ammunition, mounted their horses and rode away.

The Apache warriors reported back shortly afterward and reported that they could find only fourteen horses; one had gotten away. Crazy Legs now sent the women, with the exception of Magdalena, with one of the braves to reclothe the dead soldiers in their uniforms.

While they were away, he gathered the other braves around and motioned for Magdalena to listen also. The warriors looked surprised at this, but made no comment and seated themselves around Crazy Legs. Great Star sat at his right side and Magdalena at his left. As he laid out his plans, he told them, "Magdalena will lead the women and she and I have already discussed what she is to do once they are in Casas Grandes. I have faith that she will be a good warrior and she will prove this to you before the day is over. When the time is right, we will assist her and the other women in their retribution on those who wronged them. Now we will prepare for battle."

He looked around at his brother, "Great Star, your part in this plan is to begin now."

"Yes, my brother, Great Star answered, "I will not fail you."

"I know you won't, now be on your way and may Usen watch over you."

A lone Mexican soldier (Great Star in a Mexican uniform) galloped toward Casas Grandes. When he reached the village, he reined in his horse at the militia headquarters, dismounted, and stumbled to the porch, grabbing at the pole which supported the roof. His uniform was torn and covered with dust. He gasped for breath and two soldiers supported him. "Take me to the commander, quickly!"

Because of the commotion, the officers inside had hurried to see what was going on. One of them, Great Star noticed, was the major who had turned over the women to Crazy Legs and himself.

"Apaches!" Great Star gasped, "Apaches . . . they are attacking our soldiers . . . they need help."

"Call the men to arms!" The major turned back to Great Star after issuing his order.

The soldiers scurried about, saddling their horses and preparing their arms.

"How many?" the major asked.

"Twenty, maybe thirty," Great Star replied as his breathing became more normal.

"How far out?"

"Maybe fifteen miles from here, on the road to the mines, just before the road turns south at the fork."

"I'll need all of your militia, captain," the major told him.

The captain turned and gave orders to his aide for the men to prepare to ride out with the major's force.

"Yes sir!" the aide saluted and left on the double.

"Major, I request permission to ride with you," Great Star said.

"But you're too exhausted to ride. You'd better stay here."

"Sir, the men need all of the help they can get. Some have already been killed. I respectfully request that I be permitted to help kill those cowardly Apaches." His face showed such determination that the major reluctantly agreed. Within a few minutes the troopers had ridden out of the town and down the dusty road which led to the mines.

When the Mexican women returned from dressing the dead soldiers in their uniforms, the party of twenty-three women and eleven men moved toward Casas Grandes. At a safe distance from the village, they dismounted and proceeded on foot. The women moved cautiously in one direction and the men in another.

Before venturing any closer, the women paused to further disfigure themselves, rubbing dirt into their already disreputable countenances. "And I thought we looked pretty bad already," one of them chuckled.

They concealed themselves in an arroyo perhaps two hundred yards from the road and there they waited. At length, they saw the dust rising as a column of men rode toward them at a gallop. They sank lower into the arroyo and were still as they heard the hoof beats approach and then diminish in the distance.

The women climbed out of the arroyo and began to stagger along the road to town; they gave the appearance of having walked a long way, so slowly they walked. It wasn't long before some of the people of the village saw the faltering women, but hesitated to go to their aid, fearful of a trap. But as the women entered the village, the people gathered around them to hear what they knew of the Indian attack.

"We managed to get the keys to our shackles from the pocket of a dead soldier to free ourselves," Magdalena told them. "Thank heaven, the Apaches were too busy fighting the soldiers to pay any attention to us. Please . . . give us water," she pleaded, as some of the women fell as if exhausted, to the ground.

"But they are the ones who were sent to the mines; if we aid them, we'll be punished when the soldiers return. Put them back in the stockade and let the soldiers handle this when they return," came a yell.

"No," Magdalena protested in a weak voice. "We are not animals to be treated so; we are guilty of no wrongdoing."

"Then why were you sent to the mines?" called the same voice.

"Because we would not do what you, sir, and the rest of the officials wanted. We are not things to play with, we are wives and daughters who belong to families who love them. We are guilty of nothing but the misfortune to have been born attractive, and because of that we were taken from our families to become playthings for the officials."

"Don't listen to such nonsense," the man spoke again, "lies, all lies. They are prostitutes and criminals. Lock them up in the stockade."

A small group of well dressed men now broke through the crowd and confronted the women. "I am a judge," one of the men said as he turned to face the townspeople, "and I have found through our judicial system that some of these women are guilty of breaking the laws of our country and under the law I sentenced them, accordingly. Others of them have also been found guilty in other courts and were also sentenced. What they . . ." He was interrupted by a shout from one of the young women thus accused, "You lie . . . you stole me from my husband and my son, and when my husband tried to stop you, you ordered him killed. You weren't even man enough to kill him yourself; you had one of your corrupt henchmen do it for you. You . . . "

The judge turned quickly to the crowd and told the men around him to place the women back into the stockade, forcibly, if necessary. That if they refused, they would be guilty of treason to their country. The men hesitated, then came forward to take hold of the women, who kicked and scratched and fought each step of the way.

The judge turned and with the other officials walked back toward the government building from which they'd come. Concern could be seen on their faces and they quickened their steps.

As the men pushed the women back into their cells, one of them turned and saw the Apaches, with that horrible yellow paint under each eye, lined up with their backs flat against the inner walls of the jail. A terrified cry, a weak, inhuman sound issued from the man's mouth, but a sound loud enough for the other men to hear. In one instant all was completely still, for the Mexican men had frozen in horror as they fixed their eyes on the Apaches. Before they could recover, Crazy Legs spoke in Spanish, "One sound, one move and you will be dead men. Do you understand?"

The Mexicans raised their hands in surrender and nodded in irregular movements to show they understood only too well.

"Now lock them up, Magdalena, but have them searched first for weapons. If any of you make one sound, even a sneeze, we will come back and kill you." His grim expression was convincing if the Mexicans had needed any more persuasion.

The doors of the cells were locked and then Crazy Legs said, "Magdalena, it is your turn now."

She nodded and the women followed her out of the door and down the street toward the government building. They walked smartly, heads up, with a proud stride, thus does freedom affect the most dejected of people. The townspeople who happened to be in the street paused in astonishment as they saw the women leave the stockade building. Most of them secretly sympathized with the women and knew that their charges were probably true, but felt helpless to do anything about them. Within seconds, these timid souls were beginning to scurry for cover like a flock of doves surprised by a bird of prey. Before the women had reached the office building, the street was completely empty.

Magdalena stopped at the door of the office building and turned to glance back at the others. They said nothing, but nodded their heads as they pulled their pistols from their garments. Magdalena turned, opened the door, and followed by her companions, entered the large chamber which had a long official looking table running down its center. The officials were seated around it, apparently discussing what had just transpired. The last woman into the room slowly shut the door as the men raised their hands.

Meanwhile the Apaches swiftly loaded the rifles and other weapons and ammunition and goods on the backs of half a dozen Mexican army pack mules. They had almost completed their task when they heard the sound of laughter. Some of them looked around the corner of the barn in the direction of the laughter, while the rest brought up their mounts and finished with the packing. The laughter continued until the women came running around to the barn.

"See," Madgalena said, "we did not delay or hinder your departure in any way!"

Crazy Legs nodded approvingly and merely said, "We go now."

As the mounted women rode around the corner of the barn,

and up the street at a trot, the townspeople peered from doors and windows, but made no more other movement as they watched in fearful silence the Apaches who rode beind them, leading the heavily laden pack mules. Their calm audacity, as if they had come in to shop for supplies and were now homeward bound won a grudging admiration from some of the men who had wished to help the women, but were too fearful to try.

Magdalena had contemplated many kinds of retribution as she rode toward Casas Grandes, but had finally decided upon ridicule as a potent weapon and one less calculated to hurt the townspeople after they had departed. Accordingly, she and the other women had ordered the officials to drop their trousers after they had each been tied securely to the hitching racks which extended along the street. Each woman had then walked along the line and given each official a good blow with a willow switch stripped from the large old willow in the plaza. Twenty-three lashes for each man from the women who really warmed to their task as they progressed and laughed and cheered their followers on as they in turn went along the line. As an afterthought, eight of them repeated their blows in honor of the eight Apache women keeping watch on the outer perimeter of the village. Howls of rage and humiliation and pain soon filled the air along with the gleeful laughter of the women.

The townspeople watched with a combination of satisfaction and consternation in the knowledge that they had to continue to associate with the humiliated officials, but they discreetly remained within doors, not publicly acknowledging their passive participation in the event. It would be wise not to mention it in the future either, they well knew.

Magdalena reflected as they rode northward that she was glad they hadn't killed the officials.

The Mexican soldiers pulled their horses down into a trot to give them a breather and then they noticed the buzzards circling in the sky a few miles ahead. They resumed their gallop and before long they had reached the scene where the supposed attack had taken place.

"Oh, Holy Mother," the major breathed, as his eyes wandered over the area. "See if any are still alive," he ordered.

When all were reported to be dead, he ordered a burial detail.

"Major," Great Star interrupted with a salute, "what about

the horses?''

"Well, what about the horses?'' The major glanced around at him impatiently.

"Well, sir, while the men are dismounted, burying the dead, the Apaches could make a quick strike and drive them off.''

"Of course . . . how foolish of me. Take one man from the detail and the two of you watch the horses.''

"Yes sir.''

"You there,'' Great Star motioned to the nearest soldier, "help me herd the horses over there away from the burial detail.''

When they had the horses herded together well away from the soldiers, the Apache approached the soldier and within a flash, the soldier fell dead from his horse, and Great Star had stampeded the horses into a dead run northward. He slid to the side of his horse as he rode, making little target for the Mexican soldiers as they glanced up surprised and wondering what had caused the stampede. The major, pistol in hand, ran to his dead soldier, looked down at his face and cursed. He knew that very moment that the Apaches had once more outmaneuvered him.

The Apaches, along with the women were moving northward toward the Rio Grande River at a steady trot when they saw a cloud of dust to the south. A grunt and a nose point by one of the warriors alerted Crazy Legs. "Here comes my brother,'' he grinned.

"You're pretty close, you two, aren't you?'' Magdalena commented as Crazy Legs turned to look in the direction of the approaching dust cloud.

The Apache turned to glance at Magdalena, but did not answer. He didn't think the comment needed answering. She had a lot to learn about Apaches. Crazy Legs shouted an order to his warriors in the Apache language which Magdalena didn't understand, and five Apaches turned their horses southward to go and help Great Star.

CHAPTER THREE

T hat night as they camped, the Apaches dug a hole in the ground into which they placed a small amount of firewood. "Why the hole?" Magdalena questioned Crazy Legs.

"To hide the light, so that no one can see our campfire." He motioned to her, "Bring the women here." He drew a straight line with a stick along the ground. "You Mexicans will sit on one side of the line and we Apaches will sit facing you on the other side. We must talk. We must decide what you will do now. Tell them to come to the fire prepared to give us some answers. We wish to honor your wishes as much as possible."

They could hear the sound of horses running, and the Apache women didn't look up, but continued to prepare the sticks upon which they would roast the rabbits which the men would bring back.

The Mexican women turned in puzzlement to see the men three or four hundred yards away running their horses every which way. Some of the women laughed and some even giggled at the spectacle as they wondered if the men had lost their senses.

"What on earth has gotten into them?" Magdalena looked at Crazy Legs. "Is this some kind of Apache ritual which precedes the evening meal?" Her laughter almost rendered her question unintelligible.

Crazy Legs was not laughing, however, but stood watching the warriors.

Magdalena lowered her hands from her face as her laughter subsided and she continued, "I've never seen such behavior before. What in the world are they doing?"

"Chasing the rabbits until they are exhausted; then they can walk up to them and club them."

"How clever!"

The rabbits were skinned, cleaned, and placed over the spits to cook slowly. The Apache women wasted not a motion as they went quietly about their work and soon the aroma of the dripping fat began to whet their appetites. Nightfall had come as the Apache men took their places and the Apache women handed parcels of rabbit meat to each of them.

"Come to the fire and eat," Crazy Legs called to the Mexican women who had been seated in a circle as they discussed what they would propose to the Apaches concerning their wishes for their futures.

"Are we ready?" Magdalena looked around the circle of faces. "Everyone should be ready to express her wishes and thoughts. It will be too late tomorrow."

As the others nodded in agreement, she continued. "If anyone has any lingering doubts about anything, now is the time to speak."

"We are ready," one of them replied as they began to rise to move toward the fire.

"Then let's eat," Magdalena said, "and see what the Apaches propose."

"Or tell us," one woman whispered.

They reached the fire and seated themselves and all were silent as the Mexican women exchanged glances and then began to eat. Most of them wondered at the silence, but not one broke the quiet with a single word or sound until Crazy Legs finally spoke.

"We Apaches are Usen's children; we are the superior people, superior to all other people, whether Mexican, American, or any other Indian tribe." He pointed to the west, "Our tribal lands extend from California to the Pecos River where the sun rises, and well into your country." He looked directly at Magdalena, "We will fight to defend our country against all intruders. You may wonder why I speak of our Apache ways. I do this because I wish all of you to know and understand our ways, and because at the end of my talk, I will invite any or all of you to come with us and join our tribe. However, if you wish or have other ideas, we will honor them. You are free to choose your own destiny. I will now continue with our history as told around the Apache campfires.

"Our young are trained from the earliest age that all are enemies of the Apache. They are also taught that the Apaches live by their wits; they must outsmart, outrun, outshoot, and outmaneuver their enemies. Our people are broken into bands, each numbering from fifty to eight hundred, and war parties from these bands are continuously on the prowl, looking for prey; very seldom does one band or party know that another one could be within a few miles of it. A case in point is our meeting with our Chiricahua brothers. Because these small bands are everywhere, we know when the enemy, an individual or party of individuals crosses our land. This will give you some idea of the Apache ways, enough to help you make your decisions, that is if they have not already been made. Before you speak, I wish to make very clear that there is much more to our ways and if you need more to make your decisions, you have only to ask."

"Well," Magdalena began, "we . . . it is very difficult to say what you feel sometimes, and this is one of those times. We cannot find the words to show our true feelings. Much has happened to us so quickly and so many beliefs which we were taught about Apaches have been proven wrong, that it makes it more difficult to come to the right decision. We owe our lives to you and if it had not been for your timely arrival, we would be working in the mines this very minute, but we also have families. Some of us are married and some even have children." She looked down into the fire and then up into the sky, and finally down at her folded hands and continued, "We do not think it would be wise to return to our homes because the officials would come after us, but on the other hand, if we do not return home, the law may punish our families, seeking retribution. For this reason we have come to the conclusion that it would best if we contact our families somehow and ask them to meet us at some central, easy to reach, location and from there we can go north to New Mexico to begin our lives all over again. This probably cannot be done without asking for your help once more." She looked up at Crazy Legs, "This is difficult because we owe so much to you already. There is no way in the world that our families can repay your kindness, even in a lifetime. Our families at this moment may have felt swift punishment for our behavior and we must act quickly. We have no choice but to ask you once again for your help in giving protection to our families as they pass through Apache country. Our people are poor and have next to nothing in wealth of any kind; it would be almost impossible for them to survive unmolested in their journey to join us. We are extremely embarrassed to ask that you join us in our plight, but we cannot see any other way. They may not even make the journey through Mexico to the Apache country before the government officials have them arrested. We will understand if you are reluctant to assist us any further; we have no right to even be here telling you of our dilemma, but we feel we must fight all the odds and hope for survival as any people who have fought for life. We have spoken, Crazy Legs, now we will be silent."

It was still, with no movement on the Indian side of the line, for a long time before Crazy Legs responded. "Where do you women call your home?"

"All of us come from around the area of Villa Santiago, which is east of here."

"How many miles?"

"Sixty to seventy."

32

"Why don't you," Crazy Legs suggested to Magdalena, "ride to your village and tell one of your families your plan. Tell them of the danger they face and see if they can't contact the other families and develop a plan of their own to join you somewhere on the trail?

The Mexican women took Crazy Leg's remarks as a sign of his willingness to help them to reunite with their families.

Their emotions were quick to surface as they hugged one another, wiping the tears from their eyes.

The Apaches displayed no emotion, which is customary with them. One never knew for sure what was on an Apache's mind.

Magdalena spoke on behalf of the women once more, "How can we ever repay you for this nobleness, for your bravery, for putting yourselves in danger to ensure our well being?"

"Stop this woman's talk," Crazy Legs interrupted. "Villa Santiago is far and we have no time to waste. You go now and the rest of us will move northward. If we sit here talking, the Mexican army could overtake us if they decide to try. And besides, you will be doing us a favor also."

"How is that?" Magdalena looked surprised.

"We can use your people to cover our journey north. We and our animals will mingle with your people and their animals."

Magdalena rode all through the night, reaching her village as the sun began to show a glow in the east. Her family home was located about four miles on the west side of Villa Santiago, which enabled her to reach it undetected.

A joyous reunion was had with her mother, father, and younger sister, but was cut short because of the need to relay her message to the others. The plan decided upon was a simple one, so simple that it should draw little notice. They would take only the bare necessities, no wagons, just burros, and they would leave the village individually, even the family members would leave separately. They would all meet some five miles northwest of the village in an old cottonwood grove, and from there they would leave together. At the head of this band of refugees and their burros, there would be an individual carrying a homemade flag, a flag which the Apaches had devised so that other bands would honor the safe passage which the Mescaleros had guaranteed. An Apache rider had already gone ahead to inform their people of this flag and its significance. The flag was white with a blue lightning symbol extending from its lower left hand corner to the upper right hand corner. It was trimmed with gold fringe. Magdalena's mother made it hastily while she waited for her turn to leave for the rendezvous.

What Magdalena and her people didn't realize was that a lone Apache, unseen by anyone, observed every movement made by Magdalena as she left the Apache camp and rode southward, later watching her movements around the village of Villa Santiago. He continued to watch the people as they began to leave the village. He counted forty-one people and twenty-three burros. "All are not coming," he muttered aloud to himself, "those who do come are walking, except for a few who ride horseback. They must be the old ones." He surmised that those who stayed behind were too old or sickly for such a journey or too attached to the place of their birth to leave. There would be some in the village who had no connection with the harassed women and wouldn't feel compelled to leave. Among these there could be a traitor or two. This was of concern to Great Star as he observed the movements in and around the village.

As the people gradually began to assemble at their appointed rendezvous, he noticed a rider moving westward on the road to Casas Grandes.

"There could be the first traitor," he said half aloud. His face darkened as he squirmed over the rocks and down to his horse.

The rider raced around a small curve and saw an Apache step from behind a large boulder into the center of the road. Great Star wore only a breechclout and high moccasins which were tucked into a rawhide thong in front and back. His yellow painted face and headband marked him unmistakably as an Apache. The horror of the Mexican was evident to Great Star and he grinned as the rider whirled his horse and raced back toward his village, no doubt wondering why he hadn't been killed and hoping that he wouldn't be before he reached safety.

Great Star smiled grimly as he watched the fleeing rider. He could easily have killed him, but a live rider might be a valuable lesson to others who might have similar ideas of betrayal for some possible gain. It seemed to have worked, he decided some time later, for no one else tried to leave the village. The villagers knew why the traitor's life had been spared and heeded the warning.

Great Star continued his invisible surveillance of the long line of Magdalena's people as they headed for their meeting with his brother. He chuckled to himself as he paralleled the column at a safe distance on higher ground. "Magdalena, where are your scouts?" He muttered aloud as he watched, "I did not take you for such a fool."

Suddenly a figure could be seen running from the rear toward the front of the column. Magdalena and the man exchanged some words, after which a number of people fanned out in all directions. The Apache realized he hadn't misjudged Magdalena after all.

The two parties met well below El Paso del Norte, and as planned, the Apaches, with their animals melted into the group from Mexico, both peoples benefitting.

Above El Paso, but before reaching Mesilla, the Chiricuhua Apaches and their women made their farewells and departed westward. The Mescalero Apaches continued with the Mexicans for a few more miles and then they, too, made their farewells and headed westward, toward their stronghold in the Sierra Blanca Mountains.

The party from Mexico continued northward until they reached a location which they considered suitable for a settlement. Socorro was to the north and with Mesilla and El Paso del Norte to their south, they would have markets for their products as well as places to purchase supplies. With the Rio Grande for their source of water, they should flourish. Almost with one accord they knelt to give thanks for their deliverance.

CHAPTER FOUR

Ten thousand feet high in the Sierra Blanca Mountains, an Apache sentinel spotted Crazy Legs, Great Star, and their party as they began to climb the steep, winding trails on the slopes far below. The sentinel signaled to the village that Apaches with heavily laden pack animals were on their way up, and the women of the encampment hurried about preparing for the arrival of their warriors.

Thunderbolt, Evening Star, and their daughter, Blue Bird, were eager to see the two young men of their family after their long absence. Evening Star had anticipated their arrival three days earlier, and with the aid of her daughter, she had gathered the heart of the agave or century plant and chopped it into pieces suitable for baking in a fire pit. It had cooked slowly, and on this, the fourth day, it would be ready.

Some of the women set out tiswin, the juice of the cactus or maize which when fermented was made into a sort of ale. It was supposed that when too much of this was drunk it could cause intoxication and lead to trouble in the village, but more often it was the tequila or whiskey which was brought in that caused the problem. Evening Star was proud of the fact that neither her husband nor her sons drank of these beverages.

Blue Bird's eyes glowed with excitement as she helped her mother. Slightly taller than her mother, she was lithe and as straight as one of the young saplings which grew near their tepee. Her parents knew it wouldn't be long before one of the young men took her from them as his wife, and they would miss her sorely. She had already participated in her maiden's puberty ceremony and was thus considered eligible for marriage. Perhaps she would remain nearby after marriage, for that was allowed.

The other women of the village were equally busy in preparing for the feast and the victory dance which would follow it. The large cooking fires were built and the pots simmered over the coals at the edge of the fires. Venison and wild turkey roasted on spits and the women set out dried fruits and pots of honey to accompany their meal cakes. All was in readiness when the young boys began to run toward the west end of the camp, a signal that the warriors were about to enter the village. Each warrior would pass between the double line of boys, handing his rein to the boy who cared for his horse. This was considered a great honor to the small boys.

Great Star led the way on his paint mare. He was followed by the horse herd, and then the pack animals, and Crazy Legs brought up the rear with the warriors. Each dismounted in turn and with gravity handed over their reins and then walked to receive the congratulations of their families.

Thunderbolt showed no emotion as he saw that both of his sons were safe, but not so did Evening Star and Blue Bird greet the tall young men.

Great Star had the features of his mother, although his skin was darker and his eyes were black instead of the soft brown of his mother. He and his brother were around six feet in height, and both were lean and wiry and very agile. Their eyes danced with confidence and good health and spirits. Crazy Legs favored his father more than he did his mother, and had his father's aquiline features and long thin face, but he was taller than his father, as was Great Star. They were exceptionally good athletes and were quick to learn. Their parents had noticed in them from a very early age their great curiosity in almost everything and had taken this as a sign of intelligence.

Evening Star greeted each of her sons with dignity, but with a twinkle in her brown eyes. Her tanned skin belied her white man's heritage and her neatly plaited braids of shining brown were the only distinguishing traits to set her apart from the other Apache women. Her thin lips were quick to part in a smile and her energy was legendary, especially when it involved the care of her family. Her buckskin clothing was beautifully decorated with beadwork and she always wore the necklace which her husband had given to her. The necklace was centered with a round disk of silver with a single star as its sole decoration.

The two women and Thunderbolt, too, wore their best, most handsomely tanned buckskins, as did the others of the village. The two young men spoke to their father and hugged their mother and sister.

"We lost no warriors, my father," Crazy Legs told his father proudly.

"That is good, my son, you have proven to be a skillful leader; we are proud of you!"

The family walked to their tepee so that the two young men could also change into their best buckskins for the feast and dance.

Shortly thereafter, the drums began to beat and the singers began their chanting. This was a signal for the warriors to take their places by the fire, and when the warriors were in their places, the women and children stationed themselves behind them. It was then that the chief entered and no one sat down until he was seated. Only then did the warriors seat themselves. Now the chief raised his hands for silence and began to smoke a cigarette, blowing smoke in the four sacred directions. When he had performed this duty, he ordered the women and slaves to serve the food. Much conversation took place as they all ate, and when everyone had finished, the chief rose and asked that all be quiet. He looked to the heavens and said, "We thank You, Usen, for guiding our warriors on a successful raid. We also give thanks that through Your kindness, You saw fit to permit all of them to return to us, unharmed. For these favors, we thank You and remember You."

The chief lowered his head and sat down. He then turned to Crazy Legs and continued, "Brave warrior, son of Thunderbolt and Evening Star, tell your people of our raid into Mexico."

At the completion of Crazy Leg's description of their raid, the drums began to sound again and all danced, mimicking, and otherwise trying to duplicate the raiding party's actions against the Mexicans.

CHAPTER FIVE

T he early morning sun cast its warm rays upon the one room stone building which Steve Sommerville and Juan Hernandez called their home. Juan chopped the morning firewood while Steve fed their horses who were penned in a pole corral just a few yards from the house. An artesian spring could be heard as it bubbled in a cold, sparkling stream from the side of the nearby hill and made its way down to the forty acres of lush green pasture below the house.

The Bonito River whose headwaters began as a trickle high in the Sierra Blanca Mountains north and west of the Mescalero Apache stronghold, and about forty miles from the little rock house, meandered eastward in its snakelike fashion at the far side of the pasture. A mile or so west of the spring, the small settlement of Chozas nestled on a small plateau which overlooked the Bonito. Still farther back up the river several miles, the village of Placitas was divided by the Bonito River. Over thousands of years, the water from this river had cut from the foothills of the Sierra Blanca a fertile valley which varied in width from less than a quarter of a mile to perhaps a mile at its widest.

Steve and Juan's pasture was located at one of the wider parts of the valley. A few miles east of the spring, the Bonito, which meant pretty in Spanish, joined with the Ruidoso River whose headwaters also began high on the mountain, but southwest of the source of the Bonito. When the Ruidoso waters, meaning noisy waters in Spanish, joined with the Bonito, they combined to form the Hondo River which then continued eastward to join the waters of the Pecos.

As the two men worked, their two dogs frolicked in the brisk morning air. Andy, Steve's dog was chased by Poco, the dog belonging to Juan. Andy ran in a joyous circle, breaking his pattern now and then by reversing himself. Occasionally he dropped to the ground panting, but Poco would continue to make quick dashes at him until he would join the play once more.

A neat pile of kindling grew rapidly as Juan wielded his axe. While the horses ate from feedbags hung over their heads, Steve moved from one to another, cuffing them off with a curry comb. He automatically looked each one over for cuts or ticks as he worked.

Steve was tall and lanky, with a wisp of light brown hair escaping from under his broadrimmed hat. His blue eyes were deceptively mild on most occasions, but could turn cold and hard if he were sufficiently provoked.

Juan, on the other hand, was of medium height and build, with wavy, black hair and brown eyes. He was lithe, compact where Steve was loose-jointed. Both wore the buckskins salvaged from many a deer killed for venison. As with the Indians, they wasted nothing that they would be able to use, now or later.

Steve had come to New Mexico Territory from the McLear Ranch in Texas where he had worked as a cowpuncher. Those had been good days for Steve. He had been planning to marry the daughter of a rancher, but then in a few months, all of this changed when a new fellow moved into Big Springs and swept Stella off her feet. Steve figured Stella was better off, for the new fellow could offer Stella things which he couldn't and they could live in Big Springs, but he had been shattered at the experience, and soon he had decided to move on.

Juan had been born and lived most of his life in the village of Mesilla, near the Rio Grande River. He had worked with his father doing freighting to El Paso, and he, too, had fallen in love, planning to marry a beautiful senorita. The priest had posted the banns and all had been arranged when Juanita had been taken ill with a fever and died within days. Juan was inconsolable and was denied the philosophical solace which Steve had grasped at for comfort. One day Juanita had been happily planning their wedding and only a short time later she was lying cold and still. It wasn't fair. He could have lost her to someone else and accepted it, in time, anyway, but to know that she was taken at such a time in her young life was almost unbearable. Juan had needed to get away, and it was when he stopped to camp at the spring one twilight that he met Steve as he rode in from the west. They ate their supper together that night and decided later to throw in together, becoming trapping partners as well as guides for the army. When they were not trapping or guiding, they worked the Spring Ranch.

Andy was the first to stop playing when he saw the horse grazing down in the pasture near the cottonwoods. His ears went up and he let out a low growl and then a louder one as Poco joined in. Both dogs ran a few yards in the direction of the horse and turned back toward the men, questioningly. Juan and Steve took up their ever present rifles and walked down the slope toward the horse, their ears and eyes alert to any suspicious sound or movement.

"An Apache pony," Juan said softly.

"You're right," Steve answered, as with rifles ready they approached the pony.

"Over there," Steve pointed with his rifle at an Apache lying face up, apparently unconscious. While he knelt beside the prone warrior, Juan explored the area, looking for any other Indian sign. Steve saw that the young brave had been wounded and seemingly had lost a lot of blood. "He's near dead from loss of blood, but we might be able to do something for him," Steve panted as they carried their burden up the slope.

"I hope he had a good relationship with his God, because from what I can see, he's going to need more help than we can give him," responded Juan.

They took turns in caring for the Apache the remainder of that day and through the night, and about midmorning of the next day, the Indian slowly opened his eyes and dimly saw Steve preparing to change the bandage on his wound. He tried to raise his arm, but lacked the strength to make the effort. He made a weak sound before he again closed his eyes.

"Take it easy old boy, take it easy," Steve told him gently as he busied himself with the bandage.

It was several more hours before the Apache again opened his eyes, and this time he saw two men sitting at a table eating by the firelight. He turned his head farther and asked in a weak voice, "White eyes, why do you bother to doctor me?"

They rose and came over to the bunk. "We need an extra hand on the ranch," Steve grinned.

"How do you feel, chief?" joked Juan.

"I am not a chief," came the reply.

"Well, that may be so," Juan told him as he removed the bandage, examined the wound carefully, and then replaced the bandage, "but my friend here, and I cannot tell the difference, all we know is that you are a wounded Apache who damned near died, but luckily for you, you're going to live."

The following day the wounded youth was strong enough to tell what had happened. As he told it, he was wronged by another brave who had stolen his woman. Because he refused to accept the maid's choice of the other brave, he took him on in single combat in spite of the wishes of the chief. He had been wounded in this combat, after which the chief had banished him from the tribe for disobeying tribal law. "All I remember after I left camp was that I stopped at the creek and bathed my wound in cool water, then packed it with clean mud. The next thing I knew, I was opening my eyes here in your cabin."

"What are you called by?"

"Since I no longer belong to my Apache band, and because you both saved my life, it would be a great honor to me, as I am beginning my life over again, if you would give me a name," the Apache declared.

"What do you say, Juan? What name should we nail to his hide?"

"How do you say three in Apache?" Juan asked the Indian.

"Kah-yay."

"And what word do you use for friends?"

"Nejeunee," answered the Indian.

"Well," Juan suggested, "what do you think of Kah-yay-Nejeunee, or Three Friends?"

"That's original," Steve commented, drily.

"I like it . . . Kah-yay-Nejeunee, Kah-yay-Nejeunee, Kah-yay-Nejeunee, Kah-yay-Nejeunee," he repeated it the four sacred times.

"I'd like to call you Kah-yay for short, if that suits you," Juan added.

"Kah-yay is fine with me," the Apache said, grinning.

"Kah-yay it is, then."

"Hah," Steve said as he shook his head with a broad grin on his face, "a Mexican, a gringo, and an Apache teaming up, all woman losers; do you think we're jinxed?"

"No," answered his Indian friend, "I think the reverse is true, we will live as brothers, the way men should live and work together; it will bring us luck."

"We'll see which of you is right as time goes on," Juan told them. He extended his hand to Kah-yay's for a friendly handshake. Steve slapped Kah-yay on the back, and said, "Welcome to the Spring Ranch," as he also offered his hand to that of the Apache.

The three learned much of the ways of the Anglo, the Mexican and the Apache as they worked together in harmony.

The were busy one morning replacing a broken pole in the corral when Kah-yay yelled to his friends, "Soldiers are coming!"

Steve and Juan were removing the broken pole while Kah-yay peeled the bark from the replacement when he alerted his friends.

"I don't see any soldiers," his friends said almost simultaneously. Their eyes searched in the direction Kah-yay had indicated.

"Put your ears to the ground," Kah-yay advised them.

The other two did as he had directed and both were able to feel the vibrations. "Well, you're right about that, but how do you figure they're soldiers?" Steve asked doubtfully.

"Well, soldiers ride in formation, two by two. Listen carefully and you can hear this formation in the sounds."

When the soldiers finally rode into view, Steve drawled, "Well, I'll be . . . get down, Lieutenant Abbott," he told him as the troop halted near the corral.

"Howdy, Sommerville, Hernandez, Kah-yay," the lieutenant replied. He turned in his saddle to issue an order to his men. "I was ordered to give you a message since I was coming down this way. Major McCarthy would like to see you as soon as possible."

"What's up?"

"I'm not sure, but I think he's concerned about a party of Mexicans who are starting a new settlement south of Socorro. He received an order to check it out. You'll have to get the rest from him first hand. I don't know much more and I doubt if he does. I'd better be on my way. Adios!" He touched his hat and waved his men forward.

"Well, I guess we'd better saddle up," Juan said as he watched the cavalry trot eastward.

Steve turned to Kah-yay, saying, "That means you, too. We're a team now and where one goes, we all go. That goes for you two scallywags," he told the dogs. They sat on their haunches, smiling at him, knowing something was brewing.

They packed enough supplies on their pack horse for several days. Included in what they considered necessary was a complete Apache outfit of clothing for each man, including moccasins. A small padlike saddle was also fastened behind the pack saddle. Little Poco could ride on this if the trail became too long for the short-legged dog. The larger dog could keep up, but the small dog seemed to appreciate riding once in a while.

When the men rode away from the ranch, Kah-yay took the lead. Steve followed with the pack horse and Juan protected the rear. One could always tell when these three men were on the move, because they always took at least one pack horse, and everywhere they went the dogs were with them, also.

Within a short time, they approached Chozas, the little settlement on the plateau above the Bonito River. The people of the small hamlet were busily going about their daily lives and laughter could be heard as the small children played together. The two dogs ran ahead to greet their many small friends, and the children hugged and petted the dogs. Then the children chased the dogs who ran until finally they allowed themselves to be caught, whereupon they licked the faces of their captors.

"Buenas tardes, senors," Felix Chavez hailed them as he came toward them from the river.

"Having trouble keeping the dam in?"

"Si, and I cannot irrigate without water. It seems everytime I repair the dam, another flash flood comes down the river," complained Felix, "but I forget my manners; won't you get down and come in?"

"No thanks, Felix, we've been called to the fort, so we'd better get along up the road," Steve told him.

"Trouble?"

"Don't know," replied Juan, "the major wants to see us."

"It's not Apaches again, is it?" Felix turned to Kah-yay with a smile. "No offence, mi amigo."

The Apache merely smiled back, saying, "None taken."

"All we know at this point is that the major has a job for us. Lieutenant Abbott brought the message awhile ago."

"Si, I spoke to the lieutenant as he passed. Be careful . . I do not wish to lose such good neighbors. Adios!" Felix turned back toward the river while the men rode along the south bank up the valley.

"Senores," came a yell from some young people on the bluff. They waved their sombreros, shouting, "¿Como esta usted?" (How are you?)

"Muy bien, gracias, y usted," (Fine, thank you) came the simultaneous reply from Steve and Juan, and Kah-yay gave a wave as they settled down to a trot. The dogs had torn themselves away from their playmates and were once more trotting sedately beind the horses.

Several miles up the Bonito, the men crossed the river, pausing to water the horses and then rode on the north side of the river until they reached the outskirts of Placita. No one had spoken and each man kept his rifle cradled in his arm. Their pistols had six shells in the chambers, for this was Apache country and one didn't go unprepared and keep his hide intact for long. Just because you didn't see any Apaches, didn't mean that they weren't around, for they were past masters of the art of camouflage. An Apache could be within a dozen feet of the trail without being seen. The three men knew this well, none better than Kah-yay, and they acted accordingly. They also knew it was unlikely that Apaches would attack if you were able to respond immediately. They might follow you for miles or even days, hoping that your guard would be down for just a moment. If you were foolish enough to relax, they would strike, and you would be dead, and a little later, they would melt into the brush and rocks with all of your belongings. The Apaches seldom attacked even though they had you outnumbered, if they stood to suffer losses doing it. They had no wish to lose any men and couldn't afford to do so.

"Do you want to stop in Placitas?" Juan asked the others.

"I've no reason; how about you, Kah-yay?"

"No, let's get on to the fort and see what's on the major's mind."

They rode at a walk up the dusty street of Placitas, with the dogs close behind.

The people of the little town were going about their business briskly. Wagons moved along the street, going in both directions, as were men on horseback. Some nodded their heads politely in a silent hello and others spoke as they passed, and the loud, boisterous voice of Soto Garcia could be heard, "Hey, amigos, don't be strangers, stop by my cantina for a drink!"

"Not today, Soto, maybe next time," Juan told him.

"Muy bien," (very good) Garcia answered, with his usual broad, friendly smile.

About five or six miles above Placitas, the valley narrowed considerably and as the men approached, they became more alert, if possible, for it was an excellent place for an ambush. The sound of rocks rolling down the steep side of the canyon on their left further alerted them. They scanned the hillside and saw perhaps fifty deer standing motionless, trying to escape detection, as they watched the horsemen below. As they rode on and glanced back, they saw the deer bounding up the steep hillside. Now they rode beside a broad meadow which was intersected by the Bonito River. A few more miles brought them to the open rangeland which stretched upward toward the fort. Hills surrounded the bowl-like pasture and the men never rode that way that they didn't think what a good ranch it would make.

The fort was at the upper end of the wide grassland. Fort Stanton had no walls to protect it. The corrals and livestock buildings were constructed on the northeast side and the barracks and other buildings were built on the other three sides, with the parade ground in the center.

"There is a new settlement being constructed on the Rio Grand River not many miles south of Socorro," Major McCarthy told them after he'd welcomed them to the fort. He puffed on his

45

pipe and then continued, ''I've been ordered to check it out and I want the three of you to do the checking. What do you say? Will you take the assignment?''

''We have nothing better to do, major,'' Steve drawled. He glanced at his two partners, ''Or do we?''

''If you have nothing better to do, neither do we!'' Juan grinned.

''Good,'' the major said with satisfaction, ''report back to me as soon as you have found out what's going on up there.'' He walked to the door with them, shaking hands as he told them goodbye. He smiled ruefully, ''Frankly, I'd rather be riding with you than sitting here doing paper work, but that's the price of promotion.''

As they left the major's office, and stepped out onto the porch, the dogs who had stayed near the horses, began to growl. That could mean Apaches, as the men well knew. They usually growled at Apaches; for another danger they barked.

''We're going to have company on this trip,'' remarked Kah-yay, ''the Apaches will know of our mission before sundown. Somehow and somewhere an Apache heard our instructions and being an Apache myself, I do not intend to waste my time trying to find that scout. He has probably left the fort and is in the clear by now.''

Juan and Steve agreed as they mounted their horses and rode toward the Indian Divide.

''This new settlement is roughly eighty or ninety miles west of us,'' Steve figured.

They would be on the road for a couple of days before they reached the Rio Grande. Longer, if they didn't push too hard, and what was the hurry?

CHAPTER SIX

"What are you going to do, my brother?" asked Great Star. The two sat crosslegged in front of their small campfire. "Sommerville has orders from the soldiers to go to Magdalena's village on the Rio Grande. He has an Apache and a Mexican with him. The Apache was driven from his village in disgrace and has taken up with the white eyes."

"We will go and talk with them," Crazy Legs said. He rose and continued, "Let's you and I, my brother, prepare for a visit with the white eyes."

The two Apaches rode down Nogal Canyon, coming out below the Indian Divide. It was their intention to intercept the three men and there was no sign that they had passed that way yet, nor any sign that they were near.

"They haven't come down off Indian Divide, yet." Great Star broke the silence.

"I believe you're right, so why don't we wait back up the canyon?"

The juniper trees grew thickly where they stopped, affording an excellent source of shelter for them and their horses.

At the same moment, the three in question were descending the western side of Indian Divide. "What a view! If we were in the east, we would be overlooking several states," Steve commented. He gazed over to their left at the grandeur of the Sierra Blanca Mountains.

"Are we on a sightseeing tour?" Juan spurred ahead, "we don't want Kah-yay to get too far ahead of us and at this rate, he'll be on the plains before we make it halfway down."

When the three of them had reached the rolling plains at the bottom of the divide, they began to watch for a good place to make camp, and decided on a little benchland over Nogal Creek. It was sheltered and had water and plenty of firewood. Kah-yay, as usual, dug a small fire pit and started a small fire while Juan and Steve cared for the horses and unpacked what they needed to make camp. The dogs had been scouting around and suddenly began to growl.

"Apaches, for sure," Juan muttered, taking up his rifle.

"I don't see any," Steve said, scanning area.

"There," Kah-yay pointed with his nose toward the southeast. "Two Apaches riding toward us."

Crazy Legs and Great Star raised their hands, giving the sign of friendship as they rode to within a short distance of the camp. Steve returned the sign and so did Juan, while Kah-yay watched silently, with a stony expression and cold eyes. These were some of the people who had been so unfair, had dealt him injustice. Never again would he allow that to happen. He unconsciously slipped his finger into the trigger guard of his rifle and his eyes met those of the two other Apaches. Neither of them said a word to him or gave any indication that they wished to acknowledge him, merely giving him a quick glance as their way of saying that they knew of him. Crazy Legs looked over the other two men and said, "I see you still have the dogs. Did they warn you of our presence?"

"You didn't join us to talk of the dogs, Crazy Legs. To what do we owe your visit?" Juan gazed steadily at the young Apache. "We expected you to join us sooner, say a couple of hours back. What happened, didn't you get away from Fort Stanton soon enough? Or maybe you followed us most of the way?"

"We came to talk about the Mexican village which you are to investigate. You know that we know what your orders are, so why don't we speak freely and honestly?" Great Star suggested.

"My brother is right, why don't we begin our discussion?" Crazy Legs threw one leg over the neck of his horse and slid to the ground, always keeping his hands in full view of the three men. "We will tell you all we know of the village of the new people and why they are settling beside the Rio Grande."

"We'll welcome whatever you know about them," Juan responded.

Kah-yay kept his opinion to himself and remained aloof as the others squatted near the fire and began their discussion. When they had finished, they had learned the Apache version of where the people had come from and why they had left Mexico.

Steve thanked them for telling them and then went on, "Of course you know we'll have to ride to the village anyway, but for what it's worth, I believe you."

Crazy Legs glanced at Juan, but said nothing. Juan rose and walked to one side to confer with Steve.

"We do not wish any harm to come to these people," Great Star told them as he looked up from his seated position. "We invited them to come to our country and we hope that you people who also came to our country without our permission, will honor our words. We will be pleased if you will give this view to the major."

"We will be glad to do this upon our return to the fort," Steve promised.

"Good," said Crazy Legs, "we'll go now." They swung onto their ponies and rode into the darkness in a flash.

"Juan, do you believe them?" Kah-yay questioned.

"What do you think, Kah-yay . . . you're an Apache . . . were they telling the truth?" Juan countered.

"Yes, this time I believe them."

"Those Mexicans are lucky to have made friends of the Apaches. I'd rather have them as friends any day," Steve drawled.

"I guess it's unanimous, then," Juan commented, "I believe what they said, too."

The following morning they had eaten and were well on their way before sunup. They would ride west for several miles before skirting the malpais until they reached its narrowest width. Kah-yay knew a trail through the lava beds which Steve and Juan had never ridden. Once through the malpais, they would skirt the Oscura Mountains on the south and again turn west toward the Rio Grande.

"That's the wisest and quickest way to reach our destination if you know the way," Juan commented.

"I wonder if we'll see as many rattlesnakes over here as we did the last time?" Steve said to Juan.

"Maybe more, if we're going through the malpais. If they multiply as rapidly as people seem to, my guess is that there are plenty." His partner grinned.

The dogs trotted along beside the horses as they walked westward. They had ridden perhaps ten miles when Kah-yay pointed his nose ahead of him and grunted. Smoke could be seen and the faint sounds of gunfire could be heard.

"That's got to be the Callahan ranch," Steve said, "let's go!"

Juan yelled to the small dog to jump to his saddle and they began to race to see what the trouble was. When they had reached a knoll from which they could see the ranch, they could see the barn was on fire. They spurred down the small hill at breakneck speed toward the ranch headquarters.

"And the Indians aren't doing the attacking, either," yelled Steve as he spurred his horse on.

When they got within a few hundred yards of the ranchhouse, the outlaws broke away from their attack and rode southward, away from them, as fast as their horses could run.

Tom Callahan, rifle in hand, was joined by his wife who also carried her rifle. They ran from the house and continued to fire at the outlaws.

"They're out of rifle range, Tom," Steve shouted as he and the others pulled up and swung from their saddles before the house.

"The dirty so and so's," Tom cussed, as he looked at the cloud of dust which followed the retreat of the outlaws.

"Are you all alright?" Juan asked, just as the three Callahan kids burst from the house to join their parents. The two boys, one fourteen and his younger brother who was twelve, each carried a rifle, and ten-year-old Ann sported a pistol almost as big as she was.

Tom glanced around proudly at his family, "They'll do to ride the river with!" He looked toward the barn and shook his head.

"We'll rebuild it, Tom," his wife Charlene told him.

In the distance, Great Star and Crazy Legs waited on their ponies looking toward the Callahan ranch buildings. "Do you think the Americans got there in time to help?" Crazy Legs wondered.

His brother responded, "Yes . . . look at that cloud of dust over there, now . . . they probably have them on the run."

When the outlaws felt sure they weren't being pursued, they slowed their horses and allowed them to drink at the small seep which had collected after a recent rain. Before the men knew what had happened, two Apaches who had concealed themselves in the brush, sprang up in a surprise hail of gunfire. Three of the outlaws died instantly, and the fourth lived long enough to see Crazy Legs and Great Star both fire the shots which finished him.

"They're coming back," Tom Callahan said as he pointed to the galloping horses. But the dogs growled and Juan said, "No, Apaches."

"Take cover," Tom ordered his family, for the second time that day.

"I don't think that will be necessary," Steve told him, for he had recognized the two Apaches.

Crazy Legs and Great Star dumped the four bodies on the ground in front of the ranch house as the others looked on. "I think they belong to you," Crazy Legs said, "but we'll take their weapons and horses. They'll have no use for them, anymore." The two brothers whirled their horses and were gone in a cloud of dust.

"Friends of yours?" Tom asked quizzically.

"I guess you might say that," Steve answered doubtfully, "but in a very limited way!"

"I hope so, because I've see all kinds of Apache sign around the ranch within the past week," Tom told him soberly.

"What kind of sign?" Kah-yay asked with interest.

"The usual sign, only in larger quantities. You nearly always see signs of small raiding parties, but in the last week these signs have increased drastically. Every area of the ranch over which I have ridden lately has shown a large increase in pony tracks and I've seen enough pony tracks made by the Apaches to know them when I see them."

"Would you take us out and show us some of this sign?" Steve asked.

"Let's go; it'll take me only a minute to saddle up," replied Tom. "But we have to bury these friends of ours, first."

Their first stop was about two miles from the ranch headquarters. "There," Tom said, pointing to the partly obscured tracks of numerous barefoot ponies. "In almost any direction from here you'll see more tracks, and they all seem to be headed west."

"Something is up, and I know that when it involves Apaches, it's bad news," Juan said grimly.

I'll not take you any further; you'll have to scout around for the rest yourselves. I've a family to protect," Tom reined his horse away and headed back to the house.

"Let's follow these for awhile," suggested Kah-yay.

"Why?" asked Juan.

"Until we see added sign . . . follow me and I'll show you."

The three men walked their horses as their eyes followed the pony tracks. In about ten minutes Kah-yay stopped his horse and dismounted. Horse manure had caught the eye of the Apache, and he broke it apart with a stick.

"What are you doing?" asked Steve.

"If there's barley or oats in the manure, we could be wrong and it could be white men riding unshod horses. But the manure shows only signs of prairie grass, which means Apache. Let's go further and see if the owners of these ponies dismounted for any reason," he smiled. "Moccasin or boot prints will reinforce or disprove what we've already seen."

"Then if we find boot prints, our early evidence was not conclusive enough," commented Juan.

"That's right, it's not wise to jump to conclusions without further investigations," Kah-yay told him.

"Do you suppose Crazy Legs and Great Star knew about this, and that's why they tried to prevent us from going on to the Rio Grande to visit the new settlement?" suggested Steve. "They were afraid we'd sooner or later spot all of the sign?"

He and Juan both stiffened and looked at Kah-yay at the same time. "That means we were being set up and could mean that we're about to be surprised," Steve remarked.

"That is one of our favorite ways to get our enemy to let down its guard," Kah-yay assured them, "I should have realized it from the beginning."

"What do you mean?" asked Juan.

"Be friendly and helpful just before you strike. It almost always works. The target almost always lets down its guard."

The three men mounted hurriedly and spurred their horses in a gallop toward the Callahan ranch headquarters. "I just hope we're not too late!" Steve yelled.

Everything looked quiet as they drew near, however, and Tom was inspecting the burned out barn when they galloped into the yard.

"Inside, all of you," Steve shouted.

The three men turned their horses into a corral after quickly unsaddling them, taking their equipment to the house with them.

"No use letting the Apaches get their hands on any more than we can help," muttered Juan.

No one asked any questions as once more they closed the heavy shutters and barred the doors. Even the dogs had seemed to know that safety lay within doors and scurried in with them without being called.

"What's up?" Tom asked when everything was secured.

"We think it's a trap," Steve told him.

"We figure the Apaches are about to attack somewhere west of here and they know we have evidence of their gathering. They'll try to prevent us from alerting their victims," Juan told him, "Or at least that's the way it looks to us."

"If that's the case, maybe they'll just try to keep us pinned down until it's too late to do anything," Tom Callahan mused, as he pondered what course to take.

"I wonder how many of them there are out there," Kah-yay said, half to himself.

"Why, you can probably figure that out a lot better than any of us," Juan replied.

There was silence as each one of them watched from the loopholes constructed in each shutter.

"There's nothing out there but grass and sacaton," Tom finally declared as he turned from the window.

"If you wish to live, don't think that for a minute," Kah-yay told him in a low voice from the next window. "If we Apaches do not wish to be seen, we cannot be seen."

"What the hell is that supposed to mean?" Tom questioned in an exasperated tone.

Steve raised his rifle to his shoulder at that moment and aimed at a target.

"There's nothing out there," Tom continued, "so what are you aiming at?"

Steve squeezed the trigger and a clump of sacaton toppled over.

Tom's mouth sagged as he stared through his loophole.

"That's what I meant," Kah-yay told him.

"I believe it, I believe it," Tom's tone was considerably more subdued as he turned back to watch once more.

"We must get out of here to warn the authorities," Juan said. "I wonder what their target is. It would sure be a big help if we knew."

"How many braves do you think Crazy Legs left behind to keep us here?" Steve asked Kah-yay.

"I'd say eight or ten," his friend told him, "any more than that would amount to an insult."

"I don't believe they'll try again to get so close to the house. It's my guess that they'll keep their distance," Steve said.

"If their main objective is to keep us pinned down, then why should they risk their warriors by getting too close? It will serve their purpose just as well to remain at a distance," Kah-yay decided.

"But we can't just sit here," Juan complained, "We have to get out of here to help or at least warn of trouble."

"Is the pack horse still tied at the hitching rack at the side of the house?" Steve asked Juan, who was facing in that direction.

"Yes," and he rose, saying, "I'll do it." Before anyone had time to move, he had opened the door, was down the walk, had the pack unfastened, and was back inside with it.

"Why didn't the Apaches shoot at him, Dad?" asked one of Tom's sons.

"Because they don't want to give away their positions," came Kah-yay's quiet explanation.

Steve, Juan, and Kah-yay went into another room where they could change into Apache clothing. Next, they daubed their faces with soot from the stove.

"We'll go out and try to get rid of them . . . one way or the other," Steve said grimly. "And it'll be much easier if we're dressed as they are.''

''Kah-yay can locate them by talking in a low voice and getting them to answer. We'll try to get to them one by one under cover of the darkness. It will soon be dark enough to slip out.''

As darkness fell, they slipped out one by one through the side door and reached the cedars growing near the house on that side. The Callahans watched as best they could for any sign that the Apaches had spotted them, but the darkness which aided their friends prevented them from seeing anything from their loopholes. It seemed to them a risky business, trying to beat the Apaches at their own game, even with the help of Kah-yay.

Hours dragged by and then they heard Steve yell, ''Don't shoot; we're coming in, Tom.''

When the door had closed behind them, Tom asked, ''Do you think you got them all?''

''Yes, I think we accounted for all of them. Kah-yay got one right outside, in the cedars, and then we could only find three more besides the one in the sacaton, and Kah-yay found five horses back in the trees, so it's a safe bet that we got them all,'' Juan said with satisfaction.

''They thought that five were enough to keep us pinned down,'' Steve commented, ''but they didn't reckon with what our friend, here, taught us,'' he grinned at Kah-yay.

Charlene and her daughter bustled around the kitchen preparing a good breakfast before the Spring Ranch men rode out, and before daybreak they had saddled their horses and struck out for the Rio Grande, hoping to locate the target of the Apaches.

It was almost noon when they spotted the smoke signals. A steady cloud of smoke could be seen rising from Oscura Peak ahead of them and to their right.

''What do they say?'' Steve asked Kah-yay.

''A long continuous stream of smoke means that all Apache bands in the area are to be at a given point. That, my friend, means Crazy Legs is assembling his warriors. My guess is that they'll meet at Ojo Caliente (Hot Springs) on the Rio Grande. The smoke signal is encouraging because it does not tell the Apaches that we have been spotted, and it also means that they have not yet struck.''

''How do you know that we haven't been spotted?'' asked Juan.

''The smoke signal doesn't say that we've been spotted,'' answered Kah-yay. ''If a quick cloud of smoke rises and dissolves quickly into the air, it means that strangers are in the area, or more specifically in our case, on the plains below. If such quick clouds of smoke are repeated rapidly, this means that the strangers are numerous and heavily armed." He smiled brightly, "The same goes for fires in the darkness, but only big fires."

"I'm glad we left the dogs at the Callahans. They could use their warning of Apaches in the area better than we could," Juan commented, as he constantly searched the plains around them for any sign that Apaches were closer than on the distant peak.

"After awhile, Kah-yay pointed to the smoke signal, "Now they've spotted us!"

"Then there's no longer any need for caution. We'd better get on up the trail as fast as we can before Crazy Legs tries to head us off!"

They put their horses into a mile-eating trot. "They may have spotted us, but let's hope they haven't recognized us," Steve said.

Crazy Legs stood at the open eastern end of a semi-circle of about twenty warriors. He looked from one to another as he issued his orders. Some of the warriors had their faces covered with red clay, indicating they were not Mescaleros, but Chiricahua Apaches. These Apaches were often called Red Painted People by other branches of the scattered Apache tribes. Their most famous chief was Mangus Colorado. Crazy Legs chose this band for the job of attacking the wagon train.

The wagon train, loaded with weapons to fill a Mexican order in El Paso, had left the Feldbaumer store in Las Vegas a few days earlier. Apache scouts had watched it from the time it pulled out of Las Vegas and began its slow journey southward.

"You will go to where the Jornada del Muerto begins and then ride from there to the large grove of cottonwoods near the final watering place. It is there the attack will take place. It is there the trains stop to rest and take on water for the next ninety miles. They won't expect any trouble there and will be busy filling their water kegs and thinking about the journey before them. You will need all of the skills at your command to conceal yourselves, for upon those skills depend the success of our attack. My Mescaleros and I will attack the wagons shortly after you begin your attack. Have you any comments or questions?"

"None," came the reply from Natank-in-job (the chief

captain).

It was at this juncture that Great Star reported that three men had been spotted on the plains near Oscura Mountain, headed for Socorro, apparently.

"Use the smoke signals and ask the lookout if they travel with a pack horse and two dogs," Crazy Legs ordered. "But it couldn't be them. Clear Eyes would never let them escape from the Callahan Ranch. It must be someone else."

Three hours later, Great Star reported that the three men had no pack horse or dogs with them. "If it were the same men, they would be going to Magdalena's village instead of Socorro. Their orders were to check out the village, so it's reasonable to assume that it is not them. If there is a chance that it's them, our spies in Socorro will let us know. We will continue as planned," he concluded.

As the Spring Ranch men reached the outskirts of Socorro, Kah-yay told them to be on the alert for Apache spies in town.

"We had better not tip our hands or Crazy Legs will know before nightfall that we escaped from the Callahan ranch," Kah-yay cautioned.

"What will be our reason for being in town, then?" Juan wondered.

"How about mentioning that we are on our way to Albuquerque? We could say that we're interested in a ranch up that way," Steve suggested.

As they rode into the plaza, Juan was the first to spot the Feldbaumer wagons. Seven of them were lined up on the far side of the plaza and looked ready to roll. Each wagon had a driver with a man riding 'shotgun' seated beside him. Six men rode horseback, three in the front and three to the rear.

"That looks like a likely prospect for Crazy Legs' shopping list," drawled Steve with a grin.

"Could be," Juan grinned back, "let's check it out, but casually."

"They're not leaving though!" interrupted Kah-yay. "They look worn out . . . they just drove in." As they neared the wagons, he added, "If they'd been here long, their tracks would have been destroyed by the traffic of people and horses. They just pulled in."

"You have a pair of the most serviceable eyes in this outfit," Juan told him, "if we stick with you long enough, we may learn a little about tracking."

As they rode up alongside the wagons, they tried to determine what they might be hauling. "How's Albuquerque?"

"Bout like here," came the reply as the man prepared to step down.

"Let's get ourselves a drink to wash this dust down, Mike, what do you say?" The driver spoke to his partner.

Before they could walk away from the wagon, the wagon boss rode back along the wagons and ordered that only ten men at a time leave, and then only to eat. "There will be no drinking until we reach El Paso . . . once there you can suit yourselves. I hope you all heard me. The last ten men will go first," he yelled. "You have an hour to feed your faces!"

"I think I'm hungry," Juan said with a smile.

"I feel a little peckish, myself," Steve grinned.

The teamsters didn't feel it important to conceal their freight, and told the Spring Ranch boys about the shipment in a casual way, adding, "We have ten of the best shots in the territory riding with us, and the rest ain't too bad, either." The speaker drank the last of his coffee and rose, "With that kind of firepower, who would be crazy enough to tangle with us? We could fire enough lead in a minute to mow every blade of grass, every mesquite bush, and every other living thing clean off of the blasted ground!"

"Apaches," Steve told him with a level look.

"Hey, boss, did you hear what this jasper said?" His laughter could probably be heard all the way to Albuquerque, so loudly did he jeer.

"My name is Mathew Grady," the tall stranger in charge of the wagons told them. He pulled a chair from a nearby table and slid it next to that of Steve. "I'm responsible for these wagons and their safe delivery to the purchaser in El Paso. Now, what about Apaches?"

Steve told him what had happened to them since leaving the Spring Ranch and told him of their conclusions. "We're sure that Crazy Legs will be waiting for you somewhere between here and El Paso, and knowing him, he'll have a well planned ambush waiting for you. We didn't risk our lives to warn you just for the hell of it. You'll never make it to El Paso unless you listen to us. Crazy Legs will destroy you, for he's no fool."

"Do you think I'd let some mangy coyote of an Apache scare us off that easy? I hope they are waiting out there, for if they want to start a fight, we'll finish it . . . along with every one of them. I'm much obliged to you for the warning, though, and to show you how appreciative, your meals and drinks are on me," Grady said as he rose from his chair to leave.

"Grady, Crazy Legs is no ordinary Indian, believe me. You'll never make it to El Paso thinking that way," Steve lowered his voice, "one of your drivers told me you're hauling rifles and ammunition; you know how the Apaches would like to get their hands on that. Why don't you ask for a military escort? They'll be glad to help. If Crazy Legs sees soldiers with you, it's likely he'll back off, and if he doesn't, why then the soldiers will give you a better chance to get through," Steve concluded.

"Listen to the man," Juan advised, "we know the Mescaleros and especially Crazy Legs. He's cunning and treacherous, and one of the most deceptive Apaches alive. You won't have a chance!"

"As I told your friend here, mister, we are not afraid of Injuns. When and if they decide to attack us, we'll send them all to their happy hunting ground. Good day to you gents."

Grady turned to his men and continued, "Finish your meal, men, so the rest can fill their innards."

"He's one foolish hombre," Juan commented as they walked out of the dining room. 'With that kind of arrogance, Crazy Legs will have good hunting."

"I think we should fill the sheriff in on this whole business," Steve said, "if those men get wiped out, I want it in writing somewhere that we did the best we could to prevent it."

"Crazy Legs," Great Star said as he sat down beside his brother, "Sommerville is in Socorro and he and his partners told the wagon chief about us, but the white eyes only laughed at their warning."

"So they did escape from the Callahan Ranch. There's three good men we must never underestimate. They would make good Apaches! Our plans will not change, but we will add something to them."

The two brothers sat huddled over their plans for about half an hour, during which Crazy Legs suggested his addition. When they were finished, Great Star arose and left. Within ten minutes, he and ten other Mescaleros rode out of the camp toward Socorro.

"This will be the perfect place for our attack," Great Star told his braves. "Here are your instructions, and listen carefully, for I don't wish to lose a single one of you. The area to the east of the river is open, only mesquite, and tall grass growing there. The ground is rolling and eroded which will provide us with good cover. We'll conceal ourselves about three hundred yards from the road over there.''

When the Apaches reached an area which Great Star considered adequate, he stopped and said, ''Dismount and stuff the Apache clothing with this tall grass. When you have finished with the dummies, attach a stout stick through them from the bottom to the top.''

When the Apaches were finished with the dummies, Great Star rode back to the road and yelled, ''Show the dummies!''

He had them practice with the dummies until he was satisfied with their performance. He rode back to his warriors and said, ''This is what we're going to do. When the white eyes reach the location in the road where I stood, we will open fire with our rifles, but we will all be concealed behind these small sand hills and arroyos. On my signal, all of you will raise your dummies as we did during our practice. At different intervals, not all at once, you will pull your dummy down as though it were shot. When all of the dummies have been 'shot' we will slip down to our ponies in that deep arroyo and ride away as fast as our ponies will go, giving the white eyes the impression that we are beaten and in full retreat. They will think this is the ambush which Sommerville told them about, and if we do our job right, they will not suspect the real ambush which awaits them a few miles to the south. They should be happy with their easy win and be completely off guard when they reach our brothers.''

North of them the wagons moved in their slow, ponderous fashion along the Camino Real, headed toward Mesilla, and from there to El Paso. The three men who rode in the lead included Mathew Grady. He, along with the others cradled his rifle in his left arm, with his trigger finger ready to respond if necessary. Their eyes were alert almost to the point of being jumpy. A rabbit scurried away through the underbrush, and all three men drew a bead on it. One thing for sure, the Spring Ranch men's warning may have been only a joke back in Socorro, but it was evident it was taken seriously enough now.

The rifle crates were stacked three high in the rugged work wagons, and were lashed securely with heavy duty hemp rope. Grady halted the wagons and rode back along them, ordering each shotgun rider to move from the side of the driver to the top of the gun crates. ''This will give you an unobstructed view of the ground around you, as well as not having the driver blocking your view of the possible target behind him. Be alert men . . . it's better to be alert than sorry."

Suddenly, the air was pierced by the unmistakable sound of an arrow as it hit the back of one of the riders in the rear. He slumped over his saddle horn and then slowly slid to the ground. The other two rear guards searched the surrounding area in vain for any sign of movement.

Grady rode furiously to the rear, and then another arrow struck one of the men left to guard the front, and he, too, slid to the ground motionless. It was then that Great Star and his men began to fire, drawing the expected fire from the Americans. The dummy Apaches rose at scattered intervals and were shot down by the teamsters, who fired a steady stream of bullets until the Apache decoys didn't bob up any more. A stillness now fell while the men, rifles braced against their shoulders, searched the landscape for Apaches. None appeared for a very long five minutes, and then a cloud of dust was seen at least five hundred yards to the east of them as Great Star and his men galloped away. Each pony dragged a mesquite bush behind him, thus rendering him invisible through the ensuing dust. The teamsters were forced to fire at the receding dust to vent their fury at the departing warriors. "Damn those stinking Apaches!" shouted Grady as he bent to look at the wounded men.

"They're not wounded, boss, they're dead," came word from a man who knelt beside a body.

"Sommerville was right," Grady said, as his horse whirled in first one direction and then the other as he fought to run. With his rifle butt braced on his thigh and pointing at the sky, Grady calmed his horse and ordered the wagons stopped long enough to bury the dead.

"Sommerville was right," he conceded once more, "but we drove those devils back to their rattlesnake pits. They won't bother us anymore. We showed too much firepower for those mangy curs."

The dead men were buried and read over, and the wagons were once more rolling southward. A few miles farther south, Grady could be heard to say to his men, "We'll stop at the river over yonder to camp and give the horses a chance to rest up and have all the water they want to drink and we'll take on all the water we can carry in the water barrels and canteens."

Bullets began to fly from all directions as the teamsters were caught completely off guard. Some were getting water from the river while others led their horses to water. They dove for cover, but most of them had left their rifles leaning against a wagon wheel or a tree, or anywhere but where they should have been. With pistols in hand, they searched for something at which to shoot, finding nothing. One man at a time was struck down by the invisible Apache bullets until there were only four men left alive. These made a rush for their horses and galloped up the Camino Real at top speed. One, then another, slid from the saddle and tumbled to the ground, and only two were lucky enough to escape and live to report what had happened to their seemingly invincible force.

CHAPTER SEVEN

A tall horseman with a United States marshal's badge pinned to his leather vest rode up the Bonito River valley toward the Spring Ranch. His large Stetson cast a shadow over his face, but a bushy mustache could be seen in the shadow. He went well-armed, with two pistols on his hips in addition to the rifle in its scabbard. His lean figure sat straight in the saddle, reins in his left hand and his right rested on his thigh. Silver mounted Chihuahua spurs rode on the heels of his high boots.

The Spring Ranch dogs began to bark as the marshal rode into the open meadow. This brought their masters around the side of the rock house in short order, and all three were watching intently as the rider reined in his horse a few feet from them.

"Howdy," the marshal said, "I'm U.S. Marshal Gilbert McKenna, out of the El Paso office." He dismounted and extended a hand to each in turn.

"The coffee's on," Steve told him. "Lucky we just rode in or we'd have missed you."

As the men sat at the crude kitchen table drinking the scalding coffee, McKenna told them, "we have received many complaints about this Crazy Legs and his brother, Great Star. These complaints range from an Estalano Chavez who had his cattle rustled, to a number of other ranchers who have had horses stolen in addition to cattle and anything else loose, to the Las Vegas merchant who lost an entire wagon train of guns and ammunition on its way to El Paso. I have been ordered to put a stop to these outlaw acts and I've been told that you three are experts on these two Apaches. I've decided to begin my assignment by asking for your help. It seems the more success these two have, and they have had much, the more young Apaches try to become as much like them as possible. If we don't stop these two, the southwest could become a blazing prairie fire."

"How do you propose to do that, marshal?" Juan asked as he placed his cup on the table.

"I was hoping that your experience with them could help you to come up with some ideas; after all you're the experts on those two hombres, not me!"

"We could play Apache," Kah-yay said, without looking up.

"Now what's that supposed to mean?" Steve asked, leaning forward.

"Rig a trap, as Crazy Legs does, only this time Crazy Legs will be caught," answered the Apache.

"That might work," Juan mused, "yes, that might work."

"What kind of trap, and what would we use for bait?" The marshal's interest was aroused.

"What do Apaches like the most?" Kah-yay asked.

"Now you're talking, horses, of course!" barked McKenna.

A plan was thereupon worked out whereby a large herd of horses would be driven along the Pecos River to the southern tip of the Sacramento Mountains. They would then skirt the end of the mountain and head toward El Paso. The destination of the herd would be Fort Bliss. Thinking only a few cowboys were the custodians of the herd, the Apaches would not deign to use a complicated plan, but make a bold move to steal the horses.

"Marshal . . . Juan, Kah-yay, and I will ride across the Capitans to see if we can't recruit our friends from the S-F Ranch. They are experienced Indian fighters and former mountain men from the northern Rockies. With those six, we three, and you, we ought to be sufficient to handle Crazy Legs.

"The horses we gather in the Las Vegas country should be ranch horses, already broken. Wild horses would be harder to handle and too easy to stampede, and if by chance we need to ride some of them well, you see what I'm driving at. We'll meet you in Las Vegas in a week."

Steve, Juan, and Kah-yay saddled up early the next morning and within a few hours they pulled up in front of the Sidwell headquarters house. Sam Sidwell and his wife, Carolyn, were relaxing on the verandah when the three rode in.

"Get down and rest your weary bones, my friends!' called Sam as he and Carolyn came forward to welcome their guests, and offer them coffee.

The Spring Ranch men presented the plan which had been worked out with the marshal the day before, and asked for any suggestions.

Sam Sidwell leaned forward and said grimly, "You're right about some of these young Apaches being inspired by this Crazy Legs. A little band of them raided our horse herd just last week. The sooner we put Crazy Legs out of business, it seems to me, the better for everyone. You can count on us to lend a hand," Sam told them.

The following morning, early, Sam, Carolyn, Thor, Lone Wolf, Andrew, and Arthur were riding toward Las Vegas with the Spring Ranch contingent. Thor was an old mountain man, a long time friend of Sam and Carolyn's. He and Lone Wolf had moved to the ranch recently to live out the rest of their days among their friends. Lone Wolf was a half-breed Mandan, the son of an old friend of Thor's, a fellow mountain man. Carolyn Sidwell and two brothers, Andrew and Arthur Fredericks had been rescued by Sam after a wagon train massacre years before. All four had then followed the life of trappers for several years until they had made a stake to start a ranch of their own, in New Mexico Territory. Sam and Carolyn had fallen in love, married, and had two small children.

The horse herd was grazing on the flats west of Las Vegas, only a few miles from the Gallinas River which emptied into the Pecos about forty miles south of there. One hundred and seven horses made up the herd, good horses all of them, sure to entice Crazy Legs into action, action which would snare him into the finely laid trap prepared for him and his warriors.

The plan was to move the herd southward not far from the west bank of the Pecos River. Lone Wolf, Kah-yay, and Steve would ride point, Andrew, Arthur and Juan would protect the west flank of the herd, Carolyn and Sam would cover the east flank, and the marshal and Thor would ride drag.

The banks of the Pecos River were overgrown with cottonwood trees of various heights and beneath them grew vegetation of many kinds, from sagebrush to salt cedar. The horses would be kept well away from such potential hiding places except when necessary for them to drink. The point men would see to this and keep a sharp eye out for trouble.

All knew that Crazy Legs was no ordinary Indian, but a very capable one, who could in a matter of minutes, analyze and adapt himself to any situation. He was cautious about risking his men, but at the same time able to use his cunning to completely place his enemy at a disadvantage. They also knew that he might strike at any moment, without warning or mercy. Apaches were known for being everywhere and for knowing what everyone was doing at any time in their country. When one saw no Apaches, or even any sign at all of Apaches, any prudent person would none-the-less suspect that Apaches were not far away, studying his every move.

The Apache was the master of illusion and he had mastered the art of surprise attack. So it was that the nine men and one woman who rode with the herd knew well what they had to contend with. But they, too, were expert in many of the same areas as the Apaches, and in addition they also possessed the skills of the civilized man. They were ready and eager to match their wits against those of the Apaches, and were confident they would prevail in the end. It was purely and simply a challenge by two civilizations, represented by some of the best in each.

The point men were all dressed in buckskins, each heavily armed with rifle, pistols, and a sheath knife. Their horses walked with a brisk step as their riders rode in silence, with eyes which inspected every object and every slight movement in the terrain. This was to be the ultimate challenge, win or lose, they were going to do their best. The others were similarly armed and alert, and all that could be heard were the hoofbeats and the occasional nicker of the horses.

On their second day out, they saw three Apache warriors riding parallel to them, but perhaps five hundred yards west. The two groups watched each other from that distance, with neither moving toward each other.

"What do you reckon they're up to?" Steve looked at Kah-yay.

"They're hoping we will pursue them, thereby exposing whoever chases them to a trap. In this way they hope to whittle down our numbers a little at a time. We are too well-armed for them to attack us in an open fight. They will try to outsmart us, hoping that we will make mistakes and they will not."

"Do you agree, Lone Wolf?" Steve asked.

"That's close enough," came Lone Wolf's reply, "but I would make an added observation, and that is, that they hope to take a few horses from us at a time until they get a sizable number without losing any men. Then I believe we will see them no more."

The following day there was no further sign of the Apaches.

While plans were going forward for capturing Crazy Legs and Great Star, the pair in question were also making plans, theirs to make a trip to the Gila Mountains to replenish their supply of salt. The women and children made the necessary preparations while the men looked to their weapons. Their two hundred mile trip would include fording the Rio Grande at a crossing just north of Ojo Caliente and then journeying in a northwesterly direction until they reached the Plains of San Augustin. From there, they would follow the San Francisco River until they reached Apache Creek, where they would camp.

Apache guards were placed at strategic positions as the

Mescalero women gathered the salt from a shallow lake. At the bottom of this lake, rested large salt deposits which clung to the brown mud. When these chunks of mud were removed from the bottom of the lake and washed, the mud was dissolved, thus leaving the pure salt. The salt was then placed into containers for the trip back to their stronghold.

And, as the Mescaleros have always done, no creature of Usen would be killed during this time, or harmed in any way, during the time of the salt harvest. Any enemy who wandered near them would be safe except in case of self defense. This was the way of Usen, the way of the Apache. This process was faithfully carried out and they were preparing to leave the Gilas when one of the lookouts reported to Crazy Legs of an approaching rider in the plains below.

"In Las Vegas, the government is gathering horses to ship to Fort Bliss in El Paso," the scout told Crazy Legs when he had dismounted in front of him.

"How many horses do they expect to send?"

"At least a hundred," reported the scout, "they will follow the Pecos River instead of the Rio Grande, hoping to deceive us. They believe that the horses have a better chance of reaching Fort Bliss without being stolen if they travel south along the Pecos." The scout smiled at that supposition.

"Did you find out how many riders will be with the horses?"

"I believe not more than ten," was the reply.

Crazy Legs assigned one Apache warrior to be in charge on the way back to their stronghold and he chose six choice warriors to accompany him and his brother as they headed toward the Pecos River.

After the first day out of Las Vegas, the Apaches were in constant visual contact with the herd. They had orders from Crazy Legs to watch their every move carefully to see if any routine or pattern developed, and to watch for any weakness which could be exploited.

"It's them against us,' Crazy Legs told his brother, "those horses are the bait in a trap they have prepared for us. Fort Bliss does not get its remounts from such a far distance. The long distance of this drive is solely to give us time to try to take the horses from them. It is a game. They have thrown the gauntlet down and we have picked it up. This, my brother, will be a test. Have three of our braves ride parallel with them at a safe distance. Maybe they will entice some of the wranglers to attack them. If this happens, the rest of us will be waiting."

The three Apaches had ridden thus all day, but none of the wranglers had risen to the bait. Crazy Legs next decided to try to rustle a few horses at a time, hoping in this way to frustrate his enemy into some kind of rash action. "Great Star, I want you to ride far ahead of the herd so that you cannot be spotted; take one of the braves with you. Once there, cover the front of your body with grease, then throw dirt all over the greased part of your body. The dirt will cling to your body so that when you lie on your back, you cannot be seen. The brave that you take with you will erase all tracks and other sign so that no one will suspect that you are there. The key to your success in this venture is your location. Be sure that the herd will not be too close or they'll spook. Once the herd is near, rise up and with your rope, make a quick catch and make a dash for us. Try to drive as many other horses from the herd at the same time as you can. If any of the wranglers should chase you, we'll be ready for them. I will have an ambush set up."

Great Star was nearly one hundred per cent concealed; he moved no part of his body and even his breathing was curtailed. Though he could hear the approaching herd, as yet he could see nothing. He was fortunate in that he was downwind of the herd and his keen nose picked up the smell of horsehide. Then he heard voices, but could not distinguish what was said. The voices were probably those of the point men, and they seemed to be in their proper place, to the east of him. He congratulated himself that everything was working out. The hoofbeats became louder until he could see the horses passing just to his right. But where were the wranglers who rode on the west flank of the herd? If he made a dash for the horses and they were nearby, he would fail. And then he heard their voices as they neared and he lay absolutely still. Suddenly he looked up almost into the eyes of Andrew who was looking at the ground nearby. The three flank riders rode on by, oblivious to the prone Apache, and Great Star slowly drew a deep breath. "I will count to ten four times," he said to himself, "and then I will sit up slowly so I will not spook the horses near me. I will grab one and try as my brother has told me to stampede the others that are nearby."

He put the plan into operation, leaping to the back of a horse and managing to stampede seven others with him. He leaned to the side of his horse and followed the others as they hightailed it in the direction of the waiting Apaches.

"Where in hell did he come from?" Juan howled in frustration as he watched the horses dash westward. "I can see his heel over the back of the horse and that's all I can see. Stay here, I'll try to overtake him!" he yelled to Andrew and Arthur.

His reaction was too slow, however, and Great Star was gaining on him, putting more and more distance between them. Juan knew as well as Great Star what would happen if he followed too far, and he finally turned back from the chase toward the herd, trotting toward the other two flank men.

Within the next few miles, the same tactic was tried once again and this time five horses were taken. Crazy Legs had guessed that the wranglers would figure that same tactic wouldn't be used so soon again, and he'd been right. As carefully as the herders had scanned the landscape, once again the masters of illusion had prevailed.

The marshal and Thor decided that it was time to make camp and put their heads together. There was at least an hour's daylight left as the men and Carolyn made camp not far from the river. Some of the men remained with the herd while the others made camp and decided to catch some fish for supper. There was still plenty of jerky so Kah-yay would eat that, for Apaches did not eat fish, frogs or snakes.

That night the wranglers discussed what they could do to prevent any more such disasters as they'd suffered that day. They were not too concerned about the possibility of an attack by night, for they knew that the Apaches rarely attacked by night, for they believed that if a warrior should be killed at night he would forever live in darkness in the next world. However, they continued to patrol as if an attack were imminent.

The Apaches did not launch an outright attack, it is true, but one at a time, at safe intervals they crawled through the brush into the horse herd and led a single horse back to their campsite. When morning came, they had succeeded in stealing eight more horses, all of which the night riders did not miss until Arthur saw the tracks at sunup.

"If the nights were just a little longer," Crazy Legs chuckled, "we'd have them guarding nothing by morning!"

In rage, the marshal called his people together. "What are we to do? He's making fools of us. At this rate, Crazy Legs will have half the herd before we reach the Sacramento Mountains."

Lone Wolf suggested that they make it easier for the Apaches to steal the horses, hoping that would so boltster their confidence that their guard might be lowered. He then said he'd leave camp every night under cover of the darkness and try to locate where they were holding the stolen horses. If this could be discovered, a night attack could be made on the Apaches and an attempt be made to reclaim the horses. If they were lucky, they might capture Crazy Legs, his brother, and the others.

His idea was adopted and the following morning, Lone Wolf rode into camp, "They're holding them in a draw a few miles to the west. It has water and plenty of grass, enough for our whole herd if we're not careful," he finished, wryly.

"That may be Diamond Point Draw," Steve reflected.

"It's difficult to see till you're right on it. There are small, rolling hills east of it and where I came on it, its banks are pretty steep."

Sam suggested they make their move before sunup the next morning. "As far as I'm concerned, we've dillydallied long enough. Let's get this thing over with. I don't like this cat and mouse game."

"We're beginning to feel too much sympathy for the mouse," his wife smiled.

"What do you suggest that we do, Sam?" McKenna asked.

"Let's make a bold move . . . let's stuff our clothes with some of this prairie grass and prop them up around the campfire, a very dim campfire . . . post two riders to watch the herd, three less than usual. This may be taken as an opportunity to steal as many horses as possible and head for the hills."

His plan was adopted and it was decided that Thor and Lone Wolf would be on watch that night and when the Apaches struck, they were to disappear into the darkness, allowing them free access to the herd. The others would be on the way to Diamond Point Draw to lie in wait for the Apaches to show up.

When Crazy Legs was told that only two guarded the herd that night, he was astonished, "Where are the others?"

"Sitting around their campfire, all eight of them," was the reply.

"Where are the two night riders located?"

"One is riding around the front of the herd, the other at the rear," the scout reported.

"Huh," Crazy Legs pondered, "either they suspect we won't attack at night, or it's a trap of some sort. If it's not a trap, they may be resting for some kind of move tomorrow. I think it's more likely the last, so we'll make a run on the horses and bring back as many as we can to Diamond Point Draw. We will then take what we have and head home to the mountains."

The Apaches made a successful raid on the herd and were driving their horses into the draw as the sun peeped over the hills to the east and also the heads of the wranglers ranged along the rim of the draw. The Apaches were still on their mounts when they heard the lever action of the wranglers' rifles. As they looked at the top of the embankment, they could see the rifles braced against the shoulders of the white eyes and aimed down at them. It would be sure death if they decided to resist or make a break for it. The braves took quick glances at their leader. What will it be, their eyes were asking.

Crazy Legs slid from his pony, laid his rifle on the grass, and said in a loud voice as he looked up at the cowboys, "Our time has come . . . you are masters of the field . . . we are your prisoners."

The Apaches were searched for weapons and their hands tied behind their backs, when Crazy Legs spoke once more, "My mother once told me when I was very small that the white eyes were as numerous as the blades of grass on the plains. As many as the trees in the forests. That one day their number would overwhelm us. My mother is a white woman, you know, and is the kindest and most wise person I've ever known. My brother and I have known from our boyhood days that this very day would come for the ways of the Apache are nearing an end."

A silence followed this delivery by Crazy Legs and then the marshal addressed him quietly, "Crazy Legs, you are a prisoner of war; you and your brother will be turned over to the authorities at Fort Bliss. The rest of your braves will be set free a few miles before we reach El Paso. That much I will promise, for I am in charge until then."

All now moved southward, the Apaches under heavy guard, rode at the point of the herd, and the rest pushed the herd slowly toward El Paso. About fifty miles from the cave of bats which the white man had not yet discovered, the herd left the Pecos and turned westward to skirt the lower end of the Sacramento Mountains. Crazy Legs knew that they would be traveling between the higher Sacramento Mountains on the north and the Guadalupe mountains to the south. This was rolling, semi-desert country, with many deep, dry washes or arroyos, some as much as ten or fifteen feet deep in places. These washes were dangerous to cross during the rainy season, for flash floods often roared out of the mountains during heavy rains and filled these dry creek beds to their banks, even overflowing and flooding an even wider area upon occasion.

When the hot sun would reappear and dry the desert floor with its scorching heat, large cracked patches of yellow soil could be seen between the tufts of brass and brushy vegetation.

It was late one evening with the setting sun shining directly into their faces when Thunderbolt, with the sun at his back, led his large band of warriors out of one of these dry arroyos. The warriors extended in a long line on either side of Thunderbolt. No hostile moves were made by the well-armed Apache force, but they sat their mounts motionlessly, with rifles ready, waiting for their leader's command. Thunderbolt lightly squeezed his heels into the sides of his horse, and his horse pranced forward perhaps ten feet. He said nothing, but stared at those before him.

"He must be their chief," McKenna said softly to Thor.

"No must be about it," Thor said without taking his eyes from the stern face of Thunderbolt. "They're nothing like the Indians in the north . . . here they can take you completely by surprise whenever they choose. They came in downwind to be sure we couldn't get even a whiff of trouble. They are smart and cunning and above all brave and daring. It is my council that we let our prisoners go!"

Before any other opinions could be voiced, Crazy Legs turned to the marshal and said, "I think it is time to remove these ropes, don't you think so?" No emotion was visible on the face of the young Apache as his eyes met those of the marshal. But they seemed to be saying that the marshal and his party had been out-maneuvered and it would be a fatal notion to try anything which would give cause for his father to act.

After a long moment, the marshal reached for his knife without taking his eyes from those of Crazy Legs. They continued to glare grimly into each other's eyes without blinking until the marshal had cut the ropes which bound the young brave's wrists. It took about five minutes to free the rest of the Apache prisoners and no voice could be heard and no horses or riders moved except the marshal as he moved from one to another of his prisoners.

A small westerly breeze sprang up, blowing against the backs of the long line of warriors, and it blew their hair across their faces, but none made a move to brush it away. The same breeze blew the tails of their horse and ruffled their manes, but all were motionless until the freed Apaches walked their horses toward their brethren. Then all slowly reined their horses to the north, riding toward the Sacramento Mountains, leaving a handful of chastened Americans behind them.

CHAPTER EIGHT

T he campfire in the lodge of Thunderbolt crackled cheerfully and the shadows danced against the walls of the tepee. The sound of the wind whistling through the tops of the tall Ponderosa pines which towered over the Apaches' stronghold was fierce and made the warmth of the tepee doubly appreciated.

"Winter will soon visit us," Evening Star remarked as she added more fuel to the fire. "I wonder how deep the snow will be this year?"

"Deep enough to discourage our enemies," Thunderbolt smiled as he removed the rolled cigarette from between his lips. The tobacco was rolled in oak leaves, but if tobacco were not available, other leaves were crushed as a substitute.

Laughter could be heard in the distance and Evening Star spoke disapprovingly as she replaced the flap of the tepee. "They drink too much tiswin," she shook her head. "Tiswin has brought much hardship to the Indian."

"Mother," Crazy Legs spoke with hesitation, "Great Star and I remember what you taught us about the white eyes and we were thinking of doing some traveling to see how many of them there are and how far into our country they have moved."

"You should be thinking about taking wives instead of traveling! You are both old enough to have your own lodges and families, as Blue Bird has," their mother smiled, though she scolded.

Crazy Legs glanced at his brother, then at his father, but said nothing.

"Your mother is right," their father remarked after a few moments of silence.

"We do not want to disobey our parents, and we will not, but my brother and I have been planning our travels for many months. We wish to see and hear what the white eyes are doing and planning," Crazy Legs spoke politely but persuasively.

"What you will see and find will not make you happy, my sons," their mother said with sadness in her voice. Her eyes looked into those of Crazy Legs and then she turned her eyes to those of Great Star. "There is much sadness and discouragement to be found if you make such a journey."

"Our future must be planned and one cannot properly plan his future until he knows what the future may hold for him," Great Star answered in a low voice.

"They are right, my wife," Thunderbolt laid his hand on hers, comfortingly.

Evening Star did not answer immediately, but looked straight ahead and then began to stir the fire with a small stick. She stared into the fire as she absently moved the stick. "The end is near; I will not see my grandchildren. The Apache ways are being attacked by the ways of the white eyes and we will not be able to stop them. They are too many and too hungry for land for us to be able to prevent their onslaught. My sons, that is what you will find on your travels. I will help you to pack," her tear-filled eyes met those of her sons, "and don't tell me that you are going to stop them. If you are foolish enough to think this, try to stop the snow from falling. When you can do this, then and only then will I believe that you can stop the Americanization of our country."

The following day the two made their way down Alamo Canyon toward the Hondo River, following it eastward until it emptied into the Pecos River. When they had reached this juncture, Crazy Legs turned to his brother as their horses drank deeply of the clear, cold water and said, "well, my brother, in what direction will we travel tomorrow?"

"If we wish to find the white eyes, we should travel to Santa Fe and Las Vegas, because this is where they came first before they entered our country."

A few days afterward, as their horses walked briskly in the sharp morning breeze, Great Star said, "Two horses off to the left, my brother. But there is something wrong. They don't look natural."

They watched as the two horses spotted them and raised their heads to watch the two horsemen approach. They trotted a little way and then turned toward them once more, keeping an eye on the intruders. The Indians walked their horses slowly in the direction of the strangely acting horses because they did not want to spook them, and as they drew nearer, Great Star remarked, "They're gentle enough, or they'd have been over that rise before now."

The horses had turned to face the men and one of them nickered a greeting. "There's a man tied between them." Crazy Legs said softly as he dismounted and began to move slowly toward them. He spoke soothingly to the horses, "He could be torn apart if they stampeded." He held out his hand to the nearest horse, "Easy boy, easy, we're not going to hurt you." He continued to walk slowly until he could place an arm around the horse's neck. With the other he eased a short rope around his partner's neck. "It's all right now, come and cut this poor devil loose."

The man had been tied face downward and his head hung as he lay unconscious. Great Star cut him loose as Crazy Legs let the horses go. The two horses walked over to visit with the Apache ponies while the Indians stretched the man out on the grass. "He's still breathing," Crazy Legs said, "bring some water."

While he tried to put small amounts of water into the man's mouth, Great Star examined the man's wrists and ankles. "I don't think there are any broken bones, but he's going to be one sore hombre for a few days."

When the Mexican had regained consciousness, he told his deliverers what had transpired. A band of outlaws had driven off some of his cattle and he'd given chase, only to be captured. One of them had had a diabolical sense of humor. He'd know him if he ever saw him again!

"Well, what do you want to do? Do you want to go after the men who did this to you and teach them a lesson, an Apache lesson, or do you want to forget it?" Crazy Legs continued, "What is your name?"

"Faustino Rivera is my name," the stranger answered, "I think I'd better not go after them for now, but no, I don't intend to forget it!" He grinned in anticipation and then went on, "I live south of Las Vegas a few miles, not far from Anton Chico."

Great Star interrupted, saying in Apache, that he had a feeling that Comanches were not far away.

"What did he say?" Faustino asked with a puzzled expression.

"My brother said that Comanches are coming. They seem to be many in number. Well, Faustino, I believe that the Comanches may even the score for you, if that suits you. What do you think?"

"I don't think anyone deserves a Comanche death," Faustino said finally, as he looked at his benefactors.

"If that's your answer, we had better find your countrymen before the Comanches do," Great Star told him.

It was not difficult to follow the trail. "I'll keep my eye on the trail," Great Star said, "if you will watch for any sign of Comanches."

Within hours, they came upon the outlaws as they sat on the ground talking and laughing at what one of them had said. They had been thinking of making camp to let the cattle graze. Louis was the first to stop laughing and his sober face soon got the attention of the other two. They all stared at the two Apaches with

Faustino at their side.

"Don't be foolish enough to draw your pistols," Faustino cautioned, "if you do we will have to kill you instead of leaving you for the Comanches."

"Comanches?" Carlos Benividez jumped to his feet.

"Yes, Comanches," Faustino continued, "they're only a few miles from here, and as much as I hate you for what you did to me, I cannot leave you for them and there isn't time for me to explain why these two Apaches are with me. Get on your horses and we'll make a run for my place!"

Abandoning the cattle, they raced their horses toward Anton Chico which was close to ten miles away. About five miles out, the Comanches broke off the chase and disappeared into the vastness of the plain.

"How can we ever repay you, Senor Rivera?" Carlos reined his horse to trot.

"So it's Senor Rivera now, Carlos. This morning you had no repsect for me or my family and all you wanted was my cattle. I think it is best if you and your men ride on before I'm tempted to retaliate. Get out of here before I forget I'm a Christian, but never again, do you hear me?"

"Adios, senors," Carlos turned their horses in the direction of Las Vegas.

Crazy Legs and Great Star, together with their host, were warmly welcomed into the Rivera home by Andrea Rivera, but the three Rivera children were frightened by the two Apaches and tried to hide behind the skirts of their mother. Their father then told of what had happened since he had ridden away from the ranch house that morning. Andrea said, "We won't frighten the children by telling them of Apaches ever again! These two men saved your father's life, my little ones," she knelt and put her arms around them.

Andrea prepared their meal, a welcome meal of frijoles, enchiladas, and sopapillas. After supper while they finished their coffee, they sat a long time, talking. "My house is yours," their host told them gratefully, "it will always be so."

The two brothers told him then of their reason for having been at that particular place that day. "We know of your people and they about us. We do not have love for each other, especially when you invaded our country to the south. We have been at war with each other all of our lives and the lives of those who came before us. We will continue to fight and kill each other until one of us destroys the other or drives him from his country. There is too much hate and distrust for it to be otherwise. But tonight, the war and killing will stop and we will not hate or distrust each other for the length of our stay with you and your family. Do you agree?'' Crazy Legs asked of Faustino.

"Yes, and I would like very much for our friendship to con-. tinue into the future.''

"I'm afraid that will be in the very distant future, after we have fought our last battle with the white eyes. As you have already fought your last battle with the white eyes.''

"That is true, we have fought our last battle with the Americanos, God willing, and they have won. Now they begin to move into New Mexico and bring with them their culture and language. That is how it has been since the beginning of time. The losers have to accept the new ways of the conquerors. The Americanos whom I have met thus far are not unkind or unfair, and I truly believe that one day the Americanos, the Indians, and my people will learn to live together and become one nation. True, between now and that time, there will be much hard feeling and suffering, even hate, but we will have to learn to respect each other or be conquered by another who will exploit our differences to their own ends.

"I am convinced that one day we will all be brothers. We wish that your people would realize the futility of resisting the Americanos. They are too many and too ambitious to be driven away. They call it their Manifest Destiny, and it may very well be their turn.''

"Tell us more about these Americanos, as you call them,'' Great Star said.

"I have never been to their country, but I have heard much about it. How much of what I have heard is true, I do not know, but I'm sure I've only heard a small part of what it is really like east of here. I'll tell you what I have heard, and further, I would suggest that you go to Las Vegas and Santa Fe from here. Talk with them yourselves and see what they are like.''

He paused, deciding how to proceed. "I've heard they've invented many machines to do the work of men. Machines such as the cotton gin, the sewing machine, the steamboat, the clipper ship, the railroad train, and the telegraph.''

"Wait,'' Crazy Legs interrupted, "I do not understand your words.''

"These words were also unknown to my people until, with

patience, some Americanos took the time to explain their workings to me. My mother country did not have these new machines, as yours does not. That is why the Americanos are unbeatable. They are free to make and sell their genius to whomever wishes to buy. They can even talk to others hundreds of miles away."

"Don't take me for a fool, Faustino; I am not a child. This can be done only by Usen," Crazy Legs smiled in disbelief.

"I, too, felt insulted when the Americans told me about the railroad train, which the Indians east of here call the Iron Horse, but I found later that they told the truth."

The remainder of the evening was spent in explaining to the two Apache brothers what these new contraptions did and more or less how they worked. It was a sad evening for the Apaches, for they realized that what their mother had predicted would come true, that the Apache ways, as well as the ways of other Indians would soon come to an end. The continuous flood of Americans into the West and the neverending supply of others to follow their lead, could not be halted.

First had come the mountainman trapper, followed by traders, and the land-hungry farmers followed. Cheap or free land was too much of a magnet for these agents of opportunity to be discouraged by the fear of hostile Indians. All of the stories of the cruelties done to the white man by the Indian, did not stop or even put a dent into the American push westward. The West had become the pressure valve for all of the jobless, landless, and opportunists east of the Mississippi River. Rumors of a coming war between the states' rights advocates and the unionists loomed high on the horizon. Throw in the drive of the abolitionists to free all of the slaves into the mix, and it seemed almost inevitable that a civil war would take place.

Once it was over, the thoughtful knew that there would almost certainly be an even larger flood of the displaced, homeless, and jobless people into the West. Added to them would be the political refugees, and these multitudes would almost certainly crush all resistance to the Amercian Manifest Destiny theory. The new, young country of America could not be stopped.

Faustino told of how his country had gone to war with these new and determined adventurers over Texas, and of how the Mexican War had ended with not only the loss of Texas, but of all the lands in New Mexico, California, and Arizona, and the Mexican land north of these areas. The war had ended in a humiliating complete defeat of the Mexican forces, but Faustino also told the two

Apaches that the Americanos had a more superior system of government than the Mexicans and that, in the long run, all who lived in United States of America would be vastly better off. That if Mexico had won the war, it could have brought an end to the American system of government. As Faustino put it, it had been a dictatorial system of government against a free system. Thanks be to God that the free system had prevailed. It would have been much better for all the peoples of Mexico, Faustino thought, if the United States had kept all of Mexico, annexing it to America rather than turning it back over to the rich, upper class who had ruled the downtrodden people since Mexico had won her independence from Spain.

"The Mexican people are destined to suffer many years of hardship under this upper class. Those who lived in the territory conquered by the Americanos will be the fortunate ones. Many of the Mexican mestizoes who lived in the lower part of Mexico had wished for the United States to keep Mexico, but it was not to be."

The following morning, Mrs. Rivera served the two brothers a hearty breakfast as they prepared to ride out. Faustino had a parting word of advice for them, "If you want to find out more about the Americanos, I would suggest that you stop wearing Apache clothing and replace it with what my people wear. I believe you could easily be mistaken for Mexicans."

Accordingly, he outfitted them in the appropriate clothing for their mission, and they left the Rivera Ranch dressed as Mexicans and with two new names.

CHAPTER NINE

Crazy Legs and Great Star, calling themselves Fermin and Ramon Salas, rode in the direction of the Santa Fe Trail which entered Las Vegas northeast of the Rivera Ranch. The trail was easily discernible for the ruts were deep and several wagon widths wide. The continual wear of the wagon wheels had worn the ground down until it was a foot deeper than the surrounding grassland. When the ruts became too boggy in wet weather, new tracks paralleled the old, ever extending the width of the trail. A hundred years later, the trail would still be easily seen in areas not broken by the plow.

They rode slowly, hoping to see a wagon train coming toward them. Their riding took them further and further away from Las Vegas and out into the rolling country. The two seekers of information did not see a wagon train until their second day along the trail. The slow moving train could be seen off in the distance, the white covered conestoga wagons pulled by oxen seemed to have no end to them as it moved at what seemed a snail's pace toward the two men.

"How far do you think they are from us?" Great Star asked.

"I'd guess at least three miles," his brother estimated. "See their scouts back there? I've heard they usually travel several days ahead, scouting for water or trouble; this near Las Vegas maybe not."

"They may have spotted us, so let's give them no reason to be suspicious."

The two scouts wore buckskin clothing and both were bearded. Each cradled a rifle in an arm and wore a bowie knife in a sheath at his belt. They rode straight toward the two strangers.

"Howdy," the tallest of the two said, as he pulled his horse in alongside the walking horses of the Apaches.

"And a good day to you," responded Great Star, "are you with the train?"

Fourth trip out and we're headin' for Santa Fe," came the tall man's reply.

"My name is Ramon Salas, and this is my brother, Fermin. We have just come down through Raton Pass in hopes of finding out if what we have heard is true."

"My name is Tom Fairchild, and my side kick here answers to the moniker, Henry Sullivan."

"Pleased to make your acquaintances," Henry said as he

shook hands with the two Apaches.

"What did you hear, that brought you this far south?" asked Tom.

"We heard that we're no longer Mexican citizens, that now we are citizens of the United States. Can this be true?"

"You're right, now you are Americans."

The wagons were now only a mile or two away. They were laden with merchandise to be sold in Santa Fe. No farmers were in the train, but the two Apaches' keen eyes noticed the herd of mules which were being driven half a mile or so north of the train. These mules were beginning to supplement the smaller Mexican burro and Spanish mules as transportation and for work because they could carry larger and heavier loads.

"What do you think of those mules?" Tom asked as they drew nearer. "Shouldn't they bring a good price in Santa Fe? They can work longer and can carry a heavier load than the old tamenes of Spanish times!"

"What were tamenes?" The brothers spoke almost together as they turned to look at Tom.

"You mean to say that you never heard of the tamenes?" He shook his head. "Well, the Spaniards used people to do the hauling way back there before you were born. I've been told that you could always tell a tamene when you ran across him because he always walked in a stooped position from habitually having to carry such heavy loads. The tamene wore a wide leather belt across his forehead. It extended down his back, providing a sort of sling, into which the loads were placed. Heavy padding separated the load from the back of the tamene. Those poor souls sometimes carried as much as a horse and were so poor they wore only rags. They were beaten by their Spanish overseers as they dragged from their starting place to their destination. Nice people, some of those Spaniards were."

"We've heard of the Indians that were forced to work in the mines, but the tamenes are something new to us," Crazy Legs answered.

"Well, we could talk all day, but we'd better get back to work," Tom said. "We're supposed to be ahead of the train, not in it. It's been a pleasure to meet up with you two; hope we run into you again."

Tom and Henry waved as they spurred their horses into a lope out ahead of the approaching wagon train.

Crazy Legs and Great Star sat their horses alongside the Santa

Fe Trail and watched the wagon train pass slowly before them.

"Mother is right, there are many white eyes, too many. The future grows dimmer and dimmer by the minute for those who stand in their way," Crazy Legs commented finally. "Let's go on to Las Vegas." They reined their horses around and began to pass the wagons as they rode at a brisk trot toward the village.

Las Vegas was a typical Mexican village, constructed of adobe buildings and it was apparent that it hadn't as yet felt much impact from the influence of the Americans. As was true of most of the Mexican villages, the plaza was located in the center of the town, around which buildings and dwellings of every size and description were gathered. The streets were narrow and twisting and dusty, especially during the time of the heaviest traffic. The now famous Mexican burro could be seen everywhere. Some of them furnished transporation, while others were laden with various kinds of freight, from firewood to laundry. Without doubt, these burros furnished the local inhabitants with many services.

"Hey, amigo!" Crazy Legs called to a man who was passing. "Where is a good place to get something to eat?"

"The best place is right behind you, in Mama Maria's Chili Parlor. She serves the best chili con carne and tortillas anywhere."

"Gracias!" They tied their horses to the hitching rack in front of the little eatery, and entered the poorly ventilated, one-room eating place. The floor was hard clay, the low ceiling small cedar branches placed in a pleasing design between the usual handhewn pine logs which supported the ceiling. The furniture was of the simplest, but strongly made, crisp white curtains hung at the small windows, and everything was clean and neat.

"Over here . . . come and join us." The two Apaches heard a familiar voice and turned and saw their scouts from the wagon train seated at a corner table.

"Josephine, bring two more bowls of that good chili of yours and two more orders of tortillas, along with some more honey, for our good friends, Ramon and Fermin Salas."

"Si, senor," Josephine called. She appeared and gave a quick glance at the two Mexicans who had entered. She gave them another more searching look, seeming to sense that there was something different about these two hombres.

The tortillas were soon cooked and the girl brought steaming bowls of chili, tortillas and more honey to the table. Her hands shook as she set the bowls of food in front of Ramon and Fermin.

"What's wrong, you're shaking like a leaf?" Tom said to her.

"If I didn't know better, I'd think she'd seen an Apache," Crazy Legs remarked, as he turned in his chair and surveyed the room. "But I don't see any. If there were Apaches around, I'd also shake, for Apaches never forgive anyone who has done them a wrong. They save the worst deaths for those people," he said as he looked into the girl's face. "Have you ever had any dealings with Apaches?" He looked at Tom and Henry in inquiry.

"No, can't say that we have. As a matter of fact, we've never even seen one." Henry spoke for them both.

"Apaches have terrific memories, you know," Great Star spoke quietly. "They are taught from an early age to memorize locations, messages, their history, and especially anyone who had done them wrong. I have never heard of anyone who survived if they had done an Apache wrong. The Apaches can be patient also, and have been known to wait and wait for the right time to kill an enemy. Sometimes they will even wait for months or years to even that score, and if they should be killed before their task is completed, other Apaches take up the cause and finish it. I remember one such Apache who evened the score by tying an enemy to a wagon wheel upside down and building a fire under his head." Great Star offered this bit of information casually as he helped himself to another tortilla.

"I'll bet Josephine here has heard of such stories and more, haven't you Josephine?" He looked up into her eyes.

"Si, senor, I have heard many such stories. We Mexicans learn at an early age of what the Apaches are capable of doing. That is why we have lived here so long. We mind our own business, for one lives longer that way. Is there anything else you gentlemen would like?" She had regained her composure and turned with a smile and said, "Enjoy your meal, senores, if you dare to criticize our food, I'll report you to my Apache friends, and they'll make food of you for the vultures."

"What are you two doing in Las Vegas?" Henry asked as Josephine turned away.

"We thought as long as we were down from the hills, we'd see what Las Vegas and Santa Fe are like," answered Great Star.

"Well, if you're going to Santa Fe, why don't you ride with us tomorrow?" It's not much more than sixty miles. Have you ever been to Santa Fe?"

"No, but we'd like to see it before we leave."

"Leave? Where are you headed . . . or do you think I ask too many questions? A bad habit of mine and you don't have to answer if you don't want to." Tom grinned ruefully.

"West, I guess, we want to see what California looks like since it became part of America."

"They say that people have poured into California since gold was discovered at Sutter's Mill. They've come from all corners of the world, and in between," Henry told them with a chuckle. "We heard back in Missouri that some of the forty-niners made the trip by ship around the tip of South America from the east coast, while others sailed only to the Isthmus of Panama and then traveled overland to the Pacific Ocean. From there they catch a ship up the coast to California. The many who do not have the money to go by ship just headed westward using whatever means of transportation they could afford."

"Sounds like an interesting place to see," Crazy Legs glanced at his brother. "You say that many people have traveled to California. If that is so, then the eastern part of the country must not have many people left."

Henry and Tom exchanged glances and laughed and Tom turned to their table guests to explain, "You two really are country bumpkins, aren't you? You're not pulling our legs, are you?"

"If you mean, are we joking, no we're not. Surely there can't be many Americans left in the east?"

"My friend," Tom said after he'd swallowed another spoonful of chili, "More people come to this country from Europe every month than there are in Las Vegas and Santa Fe combined."

"Europe?" Great Star said with a puzzled look on his face, "What is Europe?"

"You're really serious! You boys really don't know what's going on beyond your mountains, do you?"

Tom turned to Henry. "Where shall we begin? These boys need some learnin'."

"We don't have that much time," grinned Henry.

"All I can say is," Tom went on, "that there are more people in the United States than all four of us can count in a year or maybe two or three or more years, and there are more people headed to this country every day. Too many, for Henry and me, which is why we came west a few years back. To put some distance between us and the crowds."

Crazy Legs and Great Star looked at each other in discouragement. "Maybe there's no need to go to California. It does not seem like the kind of place we'd like to live. We don't like crowds, either."

"Why don't you fellows join up with us and explore the west?" Henry suggested, "that's what we plan to do once this wagon train gets to Santa Fe."

"Well, that's one area we do know something about, at least the southwestern part, and we'd recommend in the strongest language that you stay out of there. That's Apache country, and they don't take kindly to anyone even crossing their country, much less exploring or settling in it," Crazy Legs told them as he gave one last glance at Josephine.

"You taking a fancy to that pretty senorita?" Tom asked, with a smile.

"She's pretty all right, but more than pretty, she's smart."

"I hope she's as smart as you think she is," Great Star grinned at his brother as he spoke softly.

"Finish up, Ramon, we have to be going," Fermin told his brother shortly.

"What's your rush?" Tom asked, "You just got here; sit a spell and rest those weary bones. When we finish here, we'll mosey over to the camp and bed down for the night."

The campfire burned brightly and the men sat near enough to warm themselves against the chill evening air. The aroma of coffee floated throughout the camp. A distant voice could be heard as it sang a soothing, gentle song to keep the mules contented. The wagons were drawn into a circle, not because of the fear of an Indian attack this particular night, but because of the value of continuing the routine.

Great Star and Crazy Legs walked from wagon to wagon, chatting with the men who sat near them. Some wagons were unattended, their drivers visiting with others. When the two Apaches had the opportunity to check out one of the wagons, they crawled beneath it, giving the appearance of calling it a day as they covered themselves with their blankets. Little by little, one by one, the men began to turn in. Coyotes could be heard calling in the distance, waiting for the wagon train to leave so they could move in to eat whatever food had been left behind.

When everyone seemed to be asleep except for the guards, Crazy Legs and Great Star slowly removed their blankets, and only Apaches could have moved thus through the darkness, undetected by anyone. Slipping into the wagon which contained rolls of brightly colored cloth, they skillfully removed four rolls and read-justed the remainder so that it appeared that the rolls had not been disturbed.

Crazy Legs mounted his horse as Great Star quietly handed him the four rolls of gingham. He placed them across his lap and they both walked their horses and went back for the mules. They took four and accomplished this with the usual Apache stealth and dispatch, and within a few minutes, two mules were being led by each man into the still New Mexico night.

When morning came, neither the cloth nor the mules were missed but there was some concern expressed over the absence of Fermin and Ramon. After some discussion, the wagoneers deter-mined that the two men had decided not to accompany them to Santa Fe after all. Nothing was suspected.

Crazy Legs and Great Star, on the contrary, had decided to precede the wagon train into Santa Fe, for they were curious to see what it looked like. As they rode into the village, they were sur-prised by the similarity between Santa Fe and Las Vegas, although Santa Fe was the larger. When they reached the plaza, they saw a large number of people gathered around a platform.

"What's happening?" Crazy Legs turned to one of the number who was leaving.

"Oh that?" He nodded back over his shoulder at the platform upon which stood the figures of several Indians. Beneath the plat-form and at one side, stood more of them, under heavy guard.

"Slave sale," came his reply as he continued on his way.

Crazy Legs and Great Star eased their horses as close as they could to the platform, but remained behind the crowd. They wat-ched for fifteen or twenty minutes and observed that beautiful young women in their teens brought higher prices than the best specimen of male. The girls brought on the average of three hun-dred and fifty dollars apiece.

"Where will these Indian slaves be taken," Great Star asked a bystander.

"Home to join the rest of the slaves."

"The rest?"

"Yes, most housholds have at least five or six slaves. It's ob-vious that you two are not from here. The slave trade has been go-ing on ever since the Spaniards conquered the territory. There must be thousands of Indians slaves around here . . . mostly Nava-jos. If your're interested in buying, don't let those slick traders push an Apache off on you. They make the worst slaves and you couldn't keep one long even if you wanted to. They're just too wild and too mean, and if they don't kill you, they'll surely escape . . . or maybe both, if you're unlucky.

"Are there Apaches among these they're selling now?"

"I doubt it, no one would want one, and besides, you don't see many for they are too hard to capture. The Utes are preferred because they're more docile, and then the Navajos are the second choice. At least that's my opinion."

"I see white prisoners at the foot of the platform, where . . . ?"

Crazy Legs was interrupted by the stranger who said, "The Americans will set them free in a few minutes and the authorities will come for them. Whoever brought this bunch didn't know that the whites would be set free and the owners not compensated, either. Those Comancheros will throw a fit when they find out, but it will do them little good. The whites will be set free, but if this were back under Mexican rule, the whites would be ransomed, not sold. They'd bring more money that way. These Comancheros came out of Texas. Down there they work hand in glove with the Comanches. The Comanches do the dirty work of capturing the merchandise and then trade them to the Comancheros for guns, ammunition, and other goods. The Mexican slaves were not ransomed back in the old days, very few, if any, most of them were sold right along with the Indians. If no one paid whatever the ransom called for, the whites were sold also but like the Apaches, were not considered a good investment. Almost always, the whites were women and children, for not many white men were taken prisoner."

"I've seen and heard enough. Let's get out of this place," Crazy Legs said. They turned their horses toward the open country which could be seen in the distance, and as they rode, they passed the first church built in New Mexico and noticed three men coming out of church.

"Do you suppose they're on their way to the slave sale?" Great Star said with a laugh. "I imagine those at the slave sale have visited this place recently. Once they leave their holy place, it seems they leave their religion in the building."

"They surely don't live their religion as Apaches do." Crazy Legs put his horse into a trot up the old sloping road. Once they had reached the outskirts of Santa Fe, Great Star spoke to his brother, "Did you see them?"

"Yes, and I figure there are four of them. How many could you see?"

"Four." Crazy Legs spoke without looking at his brother. They had ridden for perhaps five miles before Crazy Legs spoke again. "They want the mules and what they carry. Let's give them a surprise. Put a pistol in your belt and keep another one in your hand. When I give the word, fire two shots and we'll both fall from our horses, but be sure you land facing them. They will take for granted that we've been ambushed. When no one appears for our animals, they will come up. That is when we will act."

Two shots rang and the two Apaches fell from their horses, lying motionless on the ground. The four outlaws who had closed the distance between themselves and their prey, stopped their horses in surprise, waiting to see who had fired the shots. After a short wait, they decided to make a dash for the horses and the mules and then hightail it back to Santa Fe.

Crazy Legs and Great Star opened fire when the outlaws were within pointblank range. They then gathered the weapons of the outlaws, packed them on the mules, tied their horses behind the mules, and within a few minutes they continued on their journey.

"Those blue mountains far ahead of us must be the Sandias. Before we reach them, the village of Bernalillo should be just north and west of them. What do you think, should we visit that village also?"

"I say let's ride around it and Albuquerque also, and head for home," Great Star replied.

A few miles from Bernalillo, the two found a secluded spot to camp, a good place to conceal the animals and plenty of grass and water. They hobbled them and turned them loose. A few hours later, they were awakened from sound slumber by a feeling of danger. "Navajos," Great Star murmured, "damn those cowardly cousins of ours . . . they are after the animals, too. I figure maybe six or seven; what do you figure?"

"That's close enough! We'll stand up and make believe we're talking to some other Apaches. When I ask you a question, muffle your voice and answer me, and I'll do the same. Give me some yellow paint and I'll paint a yellow strip under my eyes."

Crazy Legs stood up when he believed that the Navajos were within hearing distance. Being cousins of the Apache, the Navajo language is similar to that of the Apache, although they had never been as warlike. The Apaches believed that the Navajos could not match them in intelligence, cunning, or courage, either. That two Apaches could accomplish what thirty Navajos would run from, Crazy Legs firmly believed, and he was counting on this.

"Great Star," Crazy Legs yelled in the Apache language, "where are the others . . . they said it would take them only a few minutes."

"They'll be here any second," Great Star answered. He then ran a few paces and called in a muffled voice, "I'm coming, and so are the others."

"Which one are you?" called Crazy Legs.

'Too-ah-yay-say, (Strong Swimmer) came Great Star's reply.

"Where are Gian-nah-nah-tah, (Always Ready) and the others? We need all twenty of them if our plan is to succeed!" yelled Crazy Legs, grinning to himself. He was thinking that no self-respecting Apache would ever stand around yelling this loudly under any circumstances, but these were extenuating circumstances!

One Navajo had crept closer than the others, such was his curiosity, and could see the yellow painted warriors, their faces fierce in the moonlight. That glimpse was more than enough for him, and he made as rapid a withdrawal as he could manage with safety. He met two other potential horse thieves and told them of what he had seen, and with what they'd heard, they saw no reason to doubt him. They spread out and told their friends, and with no dissenting vote they decided it would be healthier to take mules and horses from those less prepared to defend their property.

Crazy Legs and Great Star chuckled softly as they saw the tall grass move slightly as their nocturnal visitors apparently changed their minds and left without even a goodbye.

"Ish-tray-nay!" (women) Crazy Legs laughed scornfully, "All are inferior to the Apaches. It's not long till morning . . . why don't we move on? If the sun is about to go to work, why shouldn't we honor him by doing likewise?"

Accordingly, they began to roll their blankets and prepare to break camp.

CHAPTER TEN

The two Apaches rode side by side, each leading a string of horses and mules across the open country east of the Rio Grande. Ten miles up river from Albuquerque, they had begun a swing around that settlement by giving it a wide berth. Accordingly they rode eastward a few miles, then continued on their southward trek, paralleling the river as they did so.

The sky was a lovely blue that morning, a typical southwestern sky, with not a cloud from horizon to horizon. The morning air was crisp and fresh as they picked their way beneath the giant cottonwoods which bordered the river. Every now and then they startled herds of deer which browsed on the undergrowth beneath the huge trees. They either jumped to safety or froze, if they thought they were undetected. The wild turkeys would take to the air when the deer ran, knowing that danger was nearby. Occasionally a flock of ducks would become airborne as they too were startled by the riders as they rounded a bend of the river. Great Star's eyes followed the ducks as they rose in the air, circled slowly and flew ahead of them down the river. "Duck would be good for a change," he commented.

The ducks flew for perhaps half a mile and again circled to land in the shallows of the river just beyond some salt cedars which grew close to the riverbank.

The two Apaches dismounted and secured the horses and mules, stripped their clothing from their bodies and slowly slid into the small lake area which joined the river. Tall grass and cattails grew in scattered clumps in the water. The brothers cut fronds of the salt cedar and combined them with stalks of the cattails, making a sort of headdress of them. With their heads lowered as far as possible into the water, they moved closer and closer to the swimming ducks. At first the ducks were skittish, but upon finding that no particular harm seemed to be attached to the moving shrubbery they concentrated on looking for food and paid little attention, not realizing that danger lurked beneath the water.

When they were in the midst of the ducks, the hunters reached up through the water and each grabbed two ducks by the legs, pulling them swiftly under the water and holding them there until they were drowned. The other ducks finally realized that cattails and salt cedar were dangerous after all, and rose from the water in panic, probably avoiding the close proximity of cattails and salt cedar thereafter.

Crazy Legs built a small fire while Great Star cleaned the ducks and spitted them on small limbs to roast over the coals. Their meal over, they moved southward once more. They would pass around Belen as they had Albuquerque. Socorro, too, was given a wide berth and then they decided that before they turned eastward toward their stronghold, they would ride south to the village of Magdalena, her family and friends.

Apaches had a high regard for luck, believing that if they had good luck when a certain person or object were present, then that same person or object would again bring good luck.

"Magdalena brought us good luck once, why don't we go by and visit her. Maybe she'll bring us good luck again," Great Star suggested.

At that moment, Crazy Legs reined in and sat studying the ground off to their left. "Someone has passed here recently," he dismounted to examine the signs a little closer. Some of the grass had been bent toward the east and had rebounded perhaps three quarters of the way back to its upright position. The two brothers studied the grass and surrounding ground and then their eyes rose in the easterly direction toward which the grass had been bent.

"I make out three separate individuals, for there are three trails," Great Star rose and again looked toward the east. He then walked a few steps and knelt once more, "Their horses are shod, so they are white eyes."

Crazy Legs broke off a piece of mesquite which was dangling from a limb and felt of it. "There is still moisture in this, so whoever passed this way is less than a day's ride ahead of us."

"They have traveled too far, then, to be of any danger to us," Great Star commented, "they must be going to the village of Manzano, they're traveling in that direction, anyway." He looked inquiringly at his brother, "Or do you think we should follow for a few miles to make sure?"

"There's no need of that; I'm sure they're headed for Manzano. We know that there were three riders and no pack horses, because pack horses heavily laden would make a deeper print. That means they were not trappers coming from the Gila Mountain area. They could have come from Navajo country northwest of here, or they could be miners looking for pesh-klitso (gold) or pesh lickoyee (silver). These white eyes desecrate mother earth by leaving scars in their search for that yellow and white iron. Well, whoever they are, they are too far from us now to be of any danger. Let's mount up and move on."

They rode in silence until the sun was beginning to set over the mountains to their west. A campsite was carefully chosen and the animals hobbled and turned loose. Crazy Legs then dug a small hole in which Great Star would build his small fire. The night slipped by uneventfully until the hooting of an owl was heard sometime after midnight. Disturbed by this, the two threw back their blankets and began their low, moaning prayers. They continued with them for long minutes until the owl could be heard no more.

"We honor and respect you," Great Star said as he rose from a seated position and knelt, "If we have offended you, we ask for your forgiveness." His eyes searched for any sign of the ghost which the Apaches believed the hooting represented. It was quiet, but the two figures knelt in silence, their outlines silhouetted against the distant mountains, remaining in this position for a long period of time. The water in the river beside them sparkled as the moon cast its glow upon it, and only the ripple of the water could be heard above the low murmur of their voices as they spoke aloud from time to time.

When they finally arose, Great Star spoke first, "Whose spirit spoke to us and why?"

"The spirit was trying to tell us something," his brother added somberly, "maybe warning us?"

"But about what?" Great Star heard the warning of the rattlesnake at that moment, and he turned quickly, "bad medicine, big power."

The Apaches feared the power of the rattlesnake because of its poisonous venom. The rattlesnake could leave its deadly powers in the area or with you yourself, for that reason no Apaches would kill a rattlesnake or molest it in any way, but tried to appease it and coax it away from their vicinity, taking its evil powers with it. Otherwise, the snake's evil spirit could bring harm, sickness, or even death to those who harmed it.

"The ghost and then the snake, both in the same day," Crazy Legs mused, "we must pray to Usen for guidance." He once more knelt and began to pray.

Great Star joined him in the low, almost inaudible prayer to their god. They made the same prayer in each of the four directions, and when they had completed their prayer, they immediately made preparations to break camp, and for the first five miles, they kept at a steady trot, after which they slowed to a fast walk.

"It would be wise to take heed of what happened back there

and be doubly alert this day," Crazy Legs said finally.

"I believe that was the purpose for the warnings back there; we must be on the lookout for trouble, big trouble, or we'd never have received the warnings," he concluded.

As they rode on in silence, each in his own way and at a time when proper, prayed again and again for guidance, and to give thanks for the warnings. In that way they might ward off the evil spirits. Suddenly, a small pile of rocks attracted their attention in an area not given to many rocks. Whoever had placed them there had obviously had to carry them from an arroyo some distance away in order to leave a message. The two brothers dismounted to examine the rocks more closely. Only other Indians used stones thus, and it had almost certainly been other Apaches who had left a message, for they were once more in Apache country. The stones were so arranged as to look as if they'd been dropped carelessly, but an Apache knew better, there would be a message in the arrangement, and they knelt to examine more closely the formation of the stones. Most of them pointed eastward so that direction would be part of the message. "There are eleven members in the Apache party," Great Star as he pointed at the way the stones were placed. "See how the earth clings to five of the stones. They've been placed in a cluster and then there are five more in another cluster, meaning five more Apaches and then the one stone apart, or another Apache, eleven in all."

"They're in trouble and in need of assistance," Crazy Legs said, "See that uprooted stone which lies against another? The sign asking for help! And the stone which rests on the other is partially turned, which means that their raid was a failure. At least it was not a disaster, if it had been the stone would be completely turned on its back."

"My guess is that if the war party is east of here and has need of help, it could be on Chupadera Mesa, a day's ride from here."

"Let's move," Crazy Legs arose, "it will take us till nightfall to reach them."

It was dusk when they heard the first gunfire. "At least we're not too late," Great Star said as he glanced at his brother.

"For some it is too late, I'm afraid."

Night shadows were creeping slowly across the canyons as the brothers hid their horses and mules in a deep arroyo and made their way up another arroyo in the direction of the shooting. They peered through the branches of a mesquite bush which grew at the edge of an arroyo and could see the uniformed Mexican soldiers scattered among the boulders.

"What are they doing in the United States? Are the Americans and Mexicans still buying Apache scalps?" Great Star murmured to his brother.

"These Mexican soldiers won't collect any more money from Apache scalps!" Crazy Legs said grimly.

"How many do you count?" Great Star asked.

"Maybe thirty."

"They're not a match for eleven Apaches on the mesa and us down here," Great Star grinned. "Let's get to killing them."

Before they went into battle, they moved back down into the arroyo and daubed their faces with warpaint, looked at each other and nodded. They drew their knives from their scabbards, put them between their teeth and crawled in different directions. A wash just ahead of them still held water from a recent rain, and they crawled through this, plastering their bodies and clothing with the slippery clay.

"If you don't smile, I'll never see you," whispered Great Star as he crawled away from his brother. The first soldier Great Star saw as he carefully crawled into range of the Mexican camp was a dead one, lying face down, with an arrow between his shoulder blades.

"Garcia?" A pause, then another whisper, "are you there?"

"Si," Great Star whispered in return.

"Como esta usted?" (How are you?)

"Esta bien." (alright)

Great Star lay on the ground between two small knolls which had mesquite growing thickly on them. His clothing, skin, and even his face were covered with mud; even the warpaint blended into the yellow clay. He could hear the Mexican soldier approaching and then could see him through the branches of the mesquite. He was a little to the right of where Great Star had expected him, walking in a crouched position, eyes searching for Garcia, who was apparently the dead soldier. His rifle was securely grasped in both hands, his finger on the trigger. He stopped for a moment and stared around him, then slowly continued toward Great Star's position. He whispered once more for Garcia and then was sent to his maker by Great Star's swift knife. But when he slid to the ground, his finger tightened on the trigger and the report broke the stillness twice as it ricocheted from the rocks nearby.

"Chihuahua!" Great Star heard someone shout, "Watch out where you aim that rifle of yours; you almost hit me." The voice continued, "Are you alright, amigo?"

Great Star moved in the direction of the voice, and when he had gotten close enough to see the soldier, he lay still for a moment, exploring the area with his eyes. The soldier sensed that something was wrong, and he began to walk backward, rifle at the ready and eyes searching the darkness in front of him. A coyote barked and this made him even more nervous.

"Alli," (over here) Great Star spoke.

The soldier whirled in a jerky fashion, displaying his extreme nervousness. "Donde?" (where?) he whispered, as he looked about tensely, his nervous eyes trying to pierce the darkness. Sweat now began to run down his face. In a matter of seconds, he too, had gone to join his comrade on his journey from this world.

When the sun rose the next morning, it brought with it a strong wind from the west. The whistle of the wind was all which could be heard, and no movement of any kind was to be seen except for the tall grass which bent in the wind and the Mexican soldiers' horses who grazed peacefully, tails to the wind. The next sign of movement came when a Mexican officer rose and looked in all directions for any signs of his night guards, then for any sign of the Apaches. He yelled to his men to report to him and only seventeen did so. "My God," he groaned, "is this all that's left? Damn those Apache dogs. Damn their souls to hell forever. Manuel, prepare to leave this hellhole. If we stay another night, all of us will be killed. Detail some of you to bury the dead . . . we can't leave them here like this."

The Apaches lay completely concealed in their vantage points and watched as the soldiers buried their dead. The Apaches respected this last service to their comrades and let them finish in peace. They still kept watch however, until the soldiers had saddled and prepared to leave the area. When they had ridden off toward the Mexican border, the whole area resumed the peace which had been interrupted when man had arrived. When the Mexican soldiers were nothing more than a dusty haze in the distance, the Apaches rose from their scattered positions surrounding the camp and gathered at the campsite. Crazy Legs and Great Star were thanked for their assistance, and a head count showed that only one warrior had been lost.

A short time later, ten warriors rode eastward toward the Sierra Blanca stronghold of the Mescaleros. They took with them the heavily laden mules and the extra horses, to be delivered to Thunderbolt from his sons. That was their payment for the assistance which the two Mescalero Apaches had rendered.

Crazy Legs and Great Star rode southwest, toward the Rio Grande, for their planned visit to Magdalena's village.

CHAPTER ELEVEN

T he sleepy, dusty little town of Esperanza was quiet as the two Apaches entered from the north. When they were first seen, the people began to rush for the nearest buildings. When the two brothers saw what was happening, they halted their horses and shouted as loudly as they could, "Magdalena, it's Crazy Legs and Great Star! Do you hear us?"

The street of the village remained empty and still as the two Apaches sat side by side on their horses just a few yards from the first adobe building. Then a woman slipped out of the door of one of the houses near the center of the town and looked up the street at the two horsemen. She wore a drab dress which reached to the ground, but a colorful shawl was thrown over her shoulders, and a straw sombrero sat on her head. "Who are you?" she shouted.

"Crazy Legs . . . and Great Star," came the answering shouts from the horsemen.

"Mi amigos," Magdalena breathed. She began to run toward the two Apaches and they trotted their horses toward the running woman.

Magdalena had much to tell her friends, and they sat at her kitchen table and listened with interest. "The Federales are getting back at us for what we did to the government officials in Casas Grandes. My husband says that they have continued to harass our relatives who chose to stay behind. Some have even been arrested and put into prison, and some have been executed, and the others fear for what the future may bring to them. It seems that one of the officials whom we humiliated was the brother of the most feared patron in the state of Chihuahua, Senor Lorenzo Gallegos. He is very rich and what he wants he gets, even the politicians in Mexico City do his bidding. It is often said that money talks, but in Mexico it shouts, and those shouts are heard in all quarters of the government, especially on the local level.

"Just recently, a few of our relatives left Mexico for Esperanza and when Senor Gallegos got wind of it, he ordered federal troops to overtake them and bring them back dead or alive, preferably dead. Our relatives had crossed the border into the United States and believed themselves safe. Who would have believed that the patron had ordered the soldiers to enter this country, if necessary, to bring them back? But they did just that. Undetected by the United States officials, of course."

"That's why the Mexican soldiers were after our brothers at

Chupadera Mesa," Crazy Legs surmised. "Our people tangled with the soldiers and the soldiers gave chase. Our people lured them to Chupadera Mesa, and night before last we gave them a surprise and what was left of them hightailed it back to Mexico."

"You fought Mexican soldiers at Chupadera Mesa and defeated them?" Magdalena was exuberant with excitement. "What wonderful news! Antonio, tell our people that they can come out of hiding now, because the Mexican soldiers have run back to Mexico with their tails between their legs, thanks once more to our Apache friends!"

"Magdalena, we are friends of yours," Crazy Legs told her, "but we are not friends to everyone. All others who have invaded our country are sworn enemies. You are our friend because according to our laws, if we accept a favor from anyone not an Apache, which we did from you at Casas Grandes, they are considered by us as adopted members of our family, and as such, an adopted member of our tribe.

"We will defend you and the people of your village as if you lived in our village. But we have a sacred duty to do as much harm as we can, to destroy, and if possible, kill everyone else in New Mexico Territory. We have been invaded by foreign people and they are trying to take our country away from us, and we intend to fight, and if necessary, to die for our country. As much as any citizen will fight and die for his country. Do you understand that? We will fight all who do not live in this village!"

"I understand now," Magdalena said with sadness in her voice. "Why can't we all, Americanos, Apaches, and Mexicans live as one people? Why can't we build a new nation together? A new nation built on justice and equality where we can all be free?"

Crazy Legs stared ahead for a time, then spoke again. "For the time being, fighting is what we will do. Who knows what the future will bring, but any man who claims to be called a man must fight to defend his country when it has been invaded." He spoke with finality.

"I'm sorry," Magdalena spoke with sincere sympathy reflected in her tone. "There is, here in this new land, a chance to change the way the world lives, a chance that may never come again. My friends and I who live here, thanks to you, have seen and lived in a land where most people are controlled by a few. A few who have no feeling or compassion for people like myself. To them, we are relegated to a permanently inferior social status. To them, we do not have the feelings attributed to the higher caste.

We are below that, we are peons, a polite word for slave. How much more degraded can one become?

"But here in this promised land, we have a chance to change all of that. We will not fail, Crazy Legs and Great Star, no matter how many years it takes, we will not fail. One day those of my lineage and also of yours will sit in the highest offices in this new land. They will occupy important chairs of prestige in the universities, they will cure the sick, and most of all, they will not be set aside because of their color, race, or whatever creed. You see, my friends, they will be just like all the rest, they will have every kind of blood that inhabits this world running through their veins; they will be Americans. Isn't that a proud word, American?"

"You have a beautiful dream, Magdalena. May Usen help make such a dream come true for you." Crazy Legs rose from his chair. "It is time for us to go, Great Star."

"I wish you could stay longer," Magdalena said, as she also rose, "our meetings are too seldom."

CHAPTER TWELVE

T he hacienda which belonged to Lorenzo Gallegos was located in a beautiful, lush valley which was studded with hundreds of giant old trees. The dazzlingly white buildings topped with red tiled roofs were far flung and comprised a village in themselves. The stables were more elegant than were most homes in Mexico, and their occupants were of the finest Arabian blood. It was evident that it required many peons to keep the large hacienda running smoothly, and several could be seen as they went about their duties in the fields and elsewhere.

The two Apaches sat their horses high on a hill overlooking the magnificent hacienda and marveled at the affluence which it represented. "This could be the home of Usen!" Great Star spoke with awe.

"Or that of one who has control over evil," his brother amended.

"I'm afraid you're right, it's the home of evil. This man, Gallegos has much power and it's all evil."

Thoughtfully, they reined their horses away, putting the hacienda behind them as they rode toward the Sierra Madre Mountains to the west. There they planned to rest while they made plans for dealing with Gallegos. Other Apache bands had strongholds in those friendly mountains, and the Mexican soldiers were well-content to leave them unmolested.

A few miles from the ranch headquarters, Crazy Legs and Great Star saw the silhouettes of two horsemen pulling a man on foot along behind them. A rope was attached to the man's neck. Occasionally he was jerked roughly and thrown to his knees and was then dragged along while the horsemen jeered and laughed at him. After they tired of this, one of them dismounted and kicked at the recumbent figure until he struggled to his feet. The poor fellow's face was cut and bruised. He wore the typical attire of the peon, white cotton britches and shirt which now hung in shreds from his battered body. His left foot wore a tattered sandal, but his right foot was bare. His bedraggled appearance failed to rouse any pity in his captors, but rather seemed to goad them to further lengths.

"Let's ride behind the cover of these hills to that small ridge ahead of them," suggested Crazy Legs. The timbre of his voice showed his extreme anger. "Once there, we'll surprise those mighty vaqueros!"

"When are you going to learn, you pig of a peon, that no one ever runs away from the patron? He always finds those who attempt to leave and brings them back. I wouldn't want to be in your shoes when we get back!" A string of curses and an vicious jerk on the rope followed this announcement.

"What do you mean, you wouldn't want to be in his shoes? He has only one and that is just a sandal." The other vaquero laughed again at his witty remark while he aimed a kick at the peon's unprotected ribs.

"Go to hell, both of you," the peon said with some spirit. His breath came in ragged gasps and he dropped to the ground once more. "May the angels put a curse on you both. I will not stand and be dragged back there. I may as well die here as back there in that hellhole called El Escorpion Hacienda." He tried to spit at his captors, but was too weak to make the effort.

The vaquero raised his hand to strike the peon once more, saying in fury, "Why you dirty . . ."

The vaquero didn't finish his sentence or the blow, because the shadows of two men moved across the ground in front of him. His eyes widened as he looked up and saw them. Two Apaches stood proudly only a few feet away. They were dressed in the typical Apache clothing. Each wore a colorful headband which held their straight black hair, the Apache symbol of courage, securely against their heads. Finger-wide yellow painted stripes extended across each of their faces. They displayed no emotion, but stood there, motionless, staring into the eyes of the Mexicans. The vaqueros saw their fate in those cold black eyes and began to tremble, finally falling to their knees, hands folded against their chests as though praying, and begged for their lives.

"Get their horses," Crazy Legs stood as though made of stone and only his lips moved as he watched the vaqueros with scorn. The hands of each man was tied behind his back and a rope tied to his ankles and then fastened to one of the saddle horns. Before the Apaches spooked the horse to which the vaqueros were tied, they removed their boots and sombreros, then slapped the horse on the rump and yelled, and the frightened horse galloped toward the ranch headquarters, the screams of the dragging men becoming fainter as the horse disappeared from view.

"I thank you senores," the peon struggled to his feet. "I owe my life to you, which as you have seen, is not worth much."

"It is worth as much as you believe it is worth," Great Star told him.

"It may be true that it isn't worth much in this country, and even less if you live under the rule of Gallegos, but there is a place called Esperanza. There you would be worth as much as your 'fine' patron," Crazy Legs said.

"Where can one so low on the social scale as I am find such a place as Esperanza?"

"Here," Great Star said. He handed the reins of the vaquero's horse to the peon. "Take a pair of these boots and a sombrero and some of our jerky and cornmeal . . . that will keep you going until you have time to hunt. Ride north until you reach a big river. It is called the Rio Grande; follow it northward until you reach the village of Esperanza. When you get there, ask for Magdalena, and tell her we sent you. Tell her you are part of her dream."

"Part of her dream, senor? I don't understand." The battered peon had a puzzled expression on his weary face.

"She'll explain it to you," Gret Star answered.

"Who shall I say sent me?" The peon put his toe into the stirrup and pulled himself painfully into the saddle and looked down at his benefactors.

"Crazy Legs and Great Star!"

"Si, senor, I will tell her that Crazy Legs and Great Star sent me. Gracias, senores . . . adios." He kicked the sides of his horse and rode away from them, then stopped, turned in the saddle and waved. He kicked the horse once more and loped over a small hill and disappeared from view.

For the second time the two Apaches lay on a hill overlooking the far flung buildings of the Gallegos hacienda. The figure of a man appeared outside the ranchhouse. He was dressed in a beautifully tailored, light tan charro outfit trimmed in black. A highly polished concho belt was fastened around his waist and smaller conchos decorated the trousers which fit closely to their owner's slightly bowed legs. His black boots were supplied to him by the best bootmaker in all of Mexico, Carlos Luhan. But his sombrero was a work of art, in a class by itself, in a tan which matched his suit, but decorated with silver, black, and red designs which were carefully woven into an unbelievably intricate design.

The man was not old, probably in his mid forties. He wore a full black mustache. He was tall, probably six feet, and when he smiled, which was seldom, his white teeth were accented by his olive skin and black mustache.

Miguel, the segundo of El Escorpion Hacienda, listened attentively to the orders being issued to him by his patron.

"Miguel, those horses are very expensive, sired by stallions of the best blood lines. Be extra careful that they are not injured as you unload them from the train at Chihuahua City. Check each one carefully as it leaves the boxcar. We are not responsible for what happens to them on their journey to Chihuahua, but once we accept them, the seller is not responsible. Do you understand?"

"Si, I understand, senor." Miguel mounted his horse and glanced at the three vaqueros sitting their horses nearby.

"If you need more men to protect my horses other than Fernando, Pablo, and Juan, use your own judgement about how many to hire and whom. I trust you completely . . . good luck and Vaya con Dios."

"Don't worry," Miguel looked down at the patron. "We will bring the horses back safely."

The four men rode toward Chihuahua City which lay about seventy miles southeast of the ranch. What Miguel did not know was that two Apaches, having taken on the appearance of Mexican vaqueros, followed at a discreet distance. They were known once more as Ramon and Fermin Salas, but their clothing had risen in status.

Gallegos had many trusted employees on his hacienda, but Miguel was second only to the patron. He managed the hacienda's numerous cattle, horse, and sheep interests. Ignacio was second only to Miguel and was his trusted segundo. The irrigated farms of feed grains, fruit orchards, and permanent pastures were under the charge of Placido. Aristeo was assigned the responsiblity of maintaining the buildings of the hacienda. The carpenters, the blacksmiths, and the like were his province. His wife, Juana was in charge of the household, and her word was law to those who served under her and kept the house ready at all times to receive the frequent guests. Damacio was the personal servant of Gallegos, doing his bidding with alacrity. He was always within the sound of the patron's voice. Each of those mentioned had many peons to do their bidding in carrying out their duties. The patron never dealt with the peons of the hacienda personally. To him, they were subhuman creatures who lived to take care of his needs, if he in fact considered them at all.

Arriving at the railroad sidetrack where the car containing the horses had been shunted, Miguel and his vaqueros prepared to take possession of their charges. He was angered as he saw the first horse led from the boxcar. They had been instructed to wait until he arrived. The horse walked down the ramp and the man who led him looked at Miguel and inquired brusquely, "Are you from the Gallegos hacienda?" The horse he held pranced sideways and snorted, glad to be released from the confines of the small stalls. His groom crooned to him softly, patting him on the neck as he looked up at Miguel.

"Si, but these horses were not to be taken from the boxcar until I examine each one." Miguel dismounted, handing the reins to one of his vaqueros, and began to examine the horse carefully; taking an unsound horse back to his patron would cause much trouble.

The groom turned to call, "Carlos, the men from the hacienda are here!"

During the confusion of unloading the horses, Crazy Legs and Great Star moved in to help with the unloading. Miguel supposed that they had accompanied the horses, and the people who had brought the horses on the first leg of their journey, took it for granted that they were with the men from the hacienda.

Miguel was satisfied after his close scrutiny of the horses and well pleased with the excellence of their confirmation. When he had signed the papers signifying acceptance of them, the deliverers left, walking toward the main part of the city. It was then that Great Star spoke to Miguel. "Senor, my name is Ramon Salas and this is my brother, Fermin. We have been with the horses since they were born and have grown much attached to them. We would like to continue to care for them if you could see a way to give us employment in that capacity."

Miguel studied the men for a few seconds and then turning to this men, began to introduce the newcomers to them. "We could use two more good men with the horses. My patron is Senor Gallegos, the patron to you, too. You are not permitted to speak to him unless he speaks to you. You are not to question his wishes, whatever his orders. I am your superior and you'll bring all of your problems to me. You are responsible to no other. I will not tolerate insolence, laziness, tardiness, and above all, disloyalty to the patron. Can you accept those conditions?"

"Si, senor!" They accepted his conditions enthusiastically.

"Get your mounts, then, and let's start moving these horses toward the hacienda."

Ten miles from the headquarters, Crazy Legs called to the segundo, "Apaches! There's all kinds of sign!"

"We figured it was Apaches who killed Orlando and Benito. They were dragged into headquarters a while back, or I should say, what was left of them. They had been tied to Orlando's horse," Miguel explained.

"How do you know Apaches did it?"

"Because both Orlando and Benito had a bit of yellow paint smeared under their eyes," Miguel answered with anger in his voice. He looked at Crazy Legs closely, 'How do you know the sign which you saw is Apache?"

Crazy Legs answered by pointing to the ground. "The horses who made these tracks were not shod, and there are moccasin tracks here and there, also."

"There are a number of Apache bands west of here in Sierra Madres and every once in a while they come out of their strongholds and raid towns, haciendas, and travelers. They are hard to see and even harder to catch, as Orlando and Benito found out. It's best to be on good terms with God, for with Apaches near you don't know when you'll be sent to meet Him. We'd better push on."

As they entered the outer perimeter of El Escorpion Hacienda, sheep were to be seen grazing on the gramma grass and a sheepdog was lying near them. A sheep herder was in the distance, walking with his staff and two more sheepdogs accompanied him, waiting for his instructions. They were the best at what they did and that was to guard the outer fringes of the flock, making sure that none wandered too far from their guardianship. Coyotes were always on the alert for a stray and were quick to take advantage of it.

Every so often rock pens were to be seen. The shepherd used these small pens which were only a few feet in diameter, to doctor a sick charge or perhaps a ewe who was having trouble giving birth. Crazy Legs noticed the pens and asked about them.

"You don't have them in your part of the country?" Explaining their use, he continued, "Perhaps your country isn't as rocky as ours. May as well make use of your rocks, huh?"

"Ignacio!" Miguel broke off his explanations and gave his second in command instructions. "Take care of the horses . . . you know where to put them. I'll ride on to the house to report to the patron. I'm sure he'll be relieved to know that we've arrived safely with them."

Two hundred yards from the main house was a large, sunken corral. It had been dug out of a slope and was forty feet wide and twice that in length. Dry rock walls lined the sides of the corral and these were perhaps eight feet in height. A dirt ramp led down to the corral and at the end of the ramp, huge timbered gates could swing together to form the enclosure. The gates were hung on giant juniper posts with four massive hinges. It was plain that great pains had been taken to make this corral secure against almost anything. Above one side of the corral, benches were placed so that observers could see what went on in the corral below.

Gallegos and his guests could watch from his vantage point while the vaqueros trained or broke the green horses. The corral was also used as a sales ring for horses, cattle, and sheep.

Ignacio sent Juan on ahead to swing back the massive gates and he and the other vaqueros slowly eased their charges down the ramp and through the gate. When the last one had passed the gate, Ignacio himself locked it. As he did so, he looked up to see Gallegos standing above, looking the horses over with a pleased expression on his face. "Damacio, aren't they beautiful?" He spoke to his ever present servant.

"Si, my patron."

"Any problems getting them here?" He turned to Miguel, inquiringly.

"No, all went smoothly, patron."

"Bueno," Gallegos answered. "I'll look at them thoroughly in the morning." He turned back toward the house, "I think I'll have my supper in the library. Please tell my wife to join me there."

"Ignacio, we'll start to train the horses tomorrow," Miguel told him. "Show Fermin and Ramon to their quarters, to the room next to the tack room. I don't want them in the bunk house. I want them close to these horses night and day."

Meanwhile, Lorenzo was partaking of his evening meal with his wife, Serena. Juana herself served the patron with one of their favorites, chicken soup, the recipe for which had been in Serena's family for generations, as a prelude to the main course. They thanked Juana and when she had withdrawn, Serena waited until she was well out of hearing before she questioned her husband.

"Lorenzo, what news do you have from Mexico City? Is that Zapotec Indian, Benito Juarez still causing trouble?"

"Serena, my dear, ever since that peon, Juan Alvarez began his drive to rid Mexico of Santa Anna and people like ourselves, there has been nothing but trouble. We must, at all costs, keep the peon in his place. We must use every tactic and method at our disposal to crush this ridiculous movement. Can you imagine at all what would happen to this country if the peons gained control? If they made their constitution the law of Mexico? Their Plan de Ayutla, as they call it, will destroy Mexico. They have driven Santa Anna out and are temporarily running the government. One of their primary goals is to take the land which the church controls and divide it among the peons. Our recourse to this outrageous plan is to purchase the church land for ourselves, using the peons as go-betweens. If this is successful, we will then own most of the land in Mexico, and those who control the land also control the government. Once that is accomplished, we will be able to throw out this American idea of a constitution.''

''I can't believe that the church would ever relinquish her control, Lorenzo. Do you really think such a thing could come to pass?''

''There is always that, my dear. When you fight the church, as these peons have the temerity to do, you fight a strong institution which has many weapons at its disposal. The church has already announced that those who swear allegiance to this new constitution will be excommunicated. That alone, should make the peons think again. And don't forget the army . . it's on our side, also.

''Soon, Miguel and his men will travel to Chihuahua to purchase the church land which borders ours to the south. This they will cede to us, and our hacienda will be enlarged substantially. Remember, my dear, the secret to getting and keeping power is to keep the peons under our control. Always remember that, and don't allow yourself to become attached or sympathetic to the lower class, for they are expendable and have been put here on this earth to do our bidding. When one of them gets out of line, he must be punished severely as a lesson to the others.'' With this admonishment, he rang the small silver bell. ''Please bring the main couse, now, Juana.''

The peons were also talking of the revolutionary concept of owning their own land and though such an idea sounded preposterous, still it gave them something to hope for, where there had been nothing.

106

CHAPTER THIRTEEN

I t was on Wednesday of the following week that an army patrol rode into the hacienda and brought with it one of the peons who had run away three weeks earlier with the intention of joining those who followed Benito Juarez.

The following morning all of the peons on the hacienda were ordered by the patron to view the body of the unfortunate man. It hung from a limb of a big tree down by the main irrigation ditch. It had been ordered by Gallegos that the peon be hung during the night. The peons, straw hats in hand and barefooted, filed past the limp body of their compatriot. They bowed their heads, making the sign of the cross, and then moved on. None spoke and the people moved slowly past the body which twisted slightly in the morning breeze, its tattered garments fluttering gently.

As Crazy Legs and Great Star filed past with the others, they noticed, as no doubt others had also, that the peon had been severely beaten before he was hanged.

When they returned to the barns, Great Star said, "I don't think I want to stay around here much longer, do you?"

"This country is going to see much killing and suffering in the days to come," his brother said grimly. "Each side is convinced that it has all the right on its side and this unyielding position is too rigid for either to give in, to compromise. Too much has happened for the peons to place much trust in the aristocrats. Too many promises have been given and then broken. There is not any trust left, there is only hate and violence, suffering and bleeding left, and this will continue for many, many years. Let's repay Magdalena's debt and then return to Sierra Blanca. What do you say?"

"I agree . . . have you any ideas about how to go about making Gallegos pay dearly for the hardships he brought to Magdalena and continues to bring to those around him?"

"What ideas do you have?" his brother asked with a grin.

"Let's play with him . . . let's scare him and scare him again and again; let's put the fear of death into Gallegos until he is afraid of his own shadow," Great Star suggested, grimly.

They went about their chores of feeding, grooming and otherwise caring for the horses as they made their plans. They agreed that the first plan should be implemented that night.

There was only a sliver of moon showing through the clouds when gunshots were heard in the barn area. Lamps were lit immediately and men ran from their living quarters half clothed, but

107

carrying weapons of all kinds. Gallegos called angrily for Damacio as he struggled into a robe and slippers.

Crazy Legs and Great Star had implemented their first plan by releasing a few of the horses, their shots stampeding them away from the barn. They then went quickly to saddle up, to give chase. They were hastily cinching up their saddles when Miguel and the patron, along with many others, appeared at the barns.

"What happened?" The patron was out of breath and patience.

"Apaches," Crazy Legs anwered, "they took some of the horses."

Gallegos looked from Crazy Legs to Great Star as they sprang into their saddles. "Where do you think you two are going?"

"With your permission, senor, we want to get the horses back before the Apaches take them too close to the Sierra Madres. Once they reach there, we'll never get them back," Great Star answered.

"But it is night and you cannot possibly follow their trail in the darkness. We don't know how many of them there are. They will kill you."

"With your permission, patron, we would like to try," Crazy Legs said as he held his horse in check.

With a glance at Miguel, the patron told them, "In God's speed."

As they rode into the darkness, they could hear the patron order Miguel to ready the men for an early morning search. They rode for perhaps two miles before they came upon the seven horses which they had released. They were grazing peacefully and looked at the two approaching riders as though they were thinking, "Well, you set us free . . . what are you up to now?" They resumed their grazing after watching the two men for awhile. Crazy Legs and Great Star dismounted, loosened their cinches, and let their horses graze also. "It will be daylight in a couple of hours. Let's start back a little before then. The horses will be full and ready to go home," Crazy Legs said with a chuckle.

They sat on the grass making their plans for the coming days until they decided it was time to be going back. They tightened their cinches once more and rode around the little band of horses, pushing them slowly toward the headquarters. The horses went willingly, for they knew their morning oats would be waiting for them. Perhaps they wondered if they would have another outing like this again tonight.

They met Miguel and his vaqueros around the next little hill.

"We never expected to see the two of you alive, much less the horses," Miguel grinned in relief and reined his horse in beside the two Apaches.

When they reached the hacienda headquarters, they found the patron pacing near the barns in anger and frustration. At the very thought of Apaches venturing right into the domains of Gallegos, he was outraged. First the peons, and now the Apaches! What had he done to deserve this? He stared in disbelief when he saw his beloved horses safely returned. "How did you get them back? How far did you have to ride before you found them? How many Apaches were there?" His questions came in quick succession.

"The Apaches apparently did not think we would pursue them, and when they saw us, they fled," Great Star told him with satisfaction.

"Fled?" Gallegos echoed in amazement, "Why would they flee from two riders?"

"Apaches do not like to fight at night," Crazy Legs told him. And when he had told him of the Apache fear that if they were killed in darkness, they would have to remain in darkness, even in the hereafter, Gallegos muttered, "I'll have to remember that." He strode back toward the house and Damacio trotted after him.

As Crazy Legs and Great Star sat their horses looking after him, Crazy Legs said in a mocking tone, "Thank you, Ramon and Fermin for risking your lives to save my horses."

"Esta nada," Great Star added in a similarly mocking tone.

"Don't get too smart," Miguel told them as he gave the two a cold stare, "or I'll report you to the patron. I don't want to have to hang two more peons . . . not right away, anyway."

He turned to the rest of his riders, "That goes for the rest of you, too." As an added emphasis to his warning, he spurred his horse close to that of Crazy Legs and knocked him from his horse. Great Star dismounted, helping his brother to his feet, and Miguel aimed a kick at Great Star's ribs before he rode off, saying over his shoulder, "That'll teach you two some manners!"

The cold, implacable hate in the eyes of the two brothers was quickly hooded as they swung themselves into their saddles.

"Not yet, my brother, not yet," murmured Crazy Legs as they rode toward the tack room. "Gallegos comes first, then Miguel."

That night, dressed as Apaches, they entered the chicken coop, killed a chicken, and started for the big house. Opening a window quietly, they stole inside and slipped down a corridor toward the patron's bedroom. Hanging the chicken from the doorframe in the center of the doorway, they carefully closed the door and left by a window in the bedroom. Before they shut the window behind them, Crazy Legs threw a large rock against the bedroom door.

The patron stirred at the sound and then rose groggily, waking his wife in the process. He groped to the door, threw it open and started to step into the corridor. The chicken struck him in the face and he pushed it away angrily, calling for Damacio. Rushing back into his room, he saw two Apaches staring at him from outside a window. Damacio ran into the room, sidetracking the hanging chicken, asking, "Que par sa?"

Gallegos swung back to Damacio, pointing his finger in horror at the window, "Apaches!" He turned to look at the window and nothing was there.

"Apaches, patron? Where?" Damacio asked innocently.

"They were there, just outside my window," Gallegos said in a shaky voice. "Didn't you see them, too? They stood side by side with that hideous paint under their eyes. Their arms were folded across their chests and each wore a red headband. Serena, you saw them, didn't you?"

Serena, standing near the bed, looked doubtfully at her husband, and said, "Why no, my husband, I saw no Apaches, but I do see that dreadful chicken hanging in the doorway. Please take it down and get rid of it, Damacio."

"Si, senora," Damacio untied the chicken and left the room.

"Who would hang a dead chicken and why?" Serena asked of her husband.

In frustration, Gallegos shouted, "How would I know? But I'll find out. Damacio!"

"Si, patron."

"Tell Miguel, Placido, Aristeo, and Juana that I want to see them at once, in the library."

Damacio disappeared as he hurried to deliver the patron's instructions.

Gallegos interrogated each of his staff, looking for answers concerning the incident of the chicken, and the appearance and disappearance of the Apaches. They were instructed to instigate individual investigations and report back to him as soon as anything could be discovered.

The following morning the chief topic of conversation at El Escorpion Hacienda was the strange happening of the night before, and that night the Apaches appeared once more before the patron, who ordered that a guard be placed outside his bedroom window.

For two days there was no further incident until a dead chicken was found hanging in Miguel's doorway. Then an entire week passed in uneasy waiting until one day two yellow stripes were found painted across the front door of the main house. By now, everyone on the hacienda was jumpy, or almost everyone, and beginning to see Apaches everywhere.

It was Saturday morning when Placido came running to the big house and reported to the patron that he had found five chickens hanging in the big tree down by the main irrigation ditch; the same tree from which had been hung the runaway peon.

"But this time the chickens had a yellow stripe painted under each eye!"

The patron received the latest news with rage and fear. "I want to see those chickens!" he bellowed.

He and Miguel stepped out onto the verandah and he was diverted by seeing Mexican cavalry approaching. A smile crossed the face of the patron and he muttered, "Now we'll get those Apache dogs."

He walked out to greet the major and his men more enthusiastically perhaps than he'd have done ordinarily. But these were not ordinary times.

"Welcome to El Escorpion, major, get down and come in for some refreshment. Miguel, take care of his men."

"Major Luis Romero," the major introduced himself. "I've been told that you have had Apache trouble."

"Yes," replied Gallegos, "and I've been told that you're one of the best Apache fighters in the army."

"I've heard such talk," the major smiled, "and I'd like very much for you to tell me about every incident which has occurred since it began. I'll waste no more time than necessary in taking those Apaches."

The two men passed into the house, the patron leading the major to the library and ringing for Juana to have wine sent to them. The major questioned the patron closely and they talked together for perhaps an hour before the patron had the major shown to his room.

"Our midday meal is served at one o'clock, Major Romero," Juana told him as she opened the guest room door and stood to one side.

"Muy bien," the major glanced around the room appreciatively

111

as he shut the door.

The following morning the major looked out of his bedroom window and saw that it was a fine morning. He turned, smiling, to open his door to go to breakfast, and ran into the cold, dead body of a chicken which was suspended from the doorframe. He tore it down with one yank, taking it to the dining room where the patron sat sipping coffee. Throwing it to the floor, he growled, "Does this look familiar to you, senor? They weren't long in welcoming me to your accursed hacienda!"

"Damacio, remove this immediately!"

The patron looked hard at the major, "Now you see what I've been contending with, major, did you see the Apaches at your window, also?"

"If they were there, I didn't see them," the major said, more calmly. "After breakfast, I would like for you to assemble all of your peons before the house."

Gallegos called once more for Damacio and instructed him to give Miguel orders to that effect. After breakfast they strode out to the front to confront the peons. They were lined up a few feet beyond the adobe wall which enclosed the gardens of the patio. Miguel sat his horse behind them. The major, with a stern expression on his face, walked slowly along the line, his hands clasped behind his back as he looked searchingly into the eyes of each peon. Suddenly he thundered, "Which of you are pretending to be Apaches?"

The peons glanced at one another in puzzlement. Suddenly, the major grabbed one peon by his shirt front, yanked him forward, then flung him into the dust. When the peon attempted to rise, the major kicked him and once more he sprawled out in the dirt. "Well?" The major roared at the peon whom he had struck.

"Well, what, senor?" the frightened peon gazed up at the major.

"Don't play games with me, you son of a dog! I want some answers and I want them now, do you hear me? I want them now!" The major turned and continued along the line. He stopped once more staring hard at the peon in front of him, and again repeated his question, "Which of you are playing at being Apaches?"

"Not me, senor," the peon answered him as he braced himself for a blow. "And I know of none who are."

Crazy Legs and Great Star could not take their eyes from Major Romero, and their hatred built as the major moved along the line, haranguing the peons who could not fight back. Before he reached the two brothers, he turned abruptly and told Miguel to

112

dismiss the peons. He walked back to the patron who stood on the verandah watching.

"As far as I can see, Senor Gallegos, your peons would never attempt such a masquerade. You saw them . . . would such as that do such a thing? I think not. My men and I will have to concentrate elsewhere to find the culprits."

Consequently, the major spent the biggest part of the day in formulating plans to trap the guilty ones, and that evening after supper, he and the patron sat long over their brandy and cigars. The library fire burned brightly as the two men discussed the ever present political situation in their country. The major looked into his glass for long moments, and then turned to look at Gallegos.

"We creoles gave birth to Mexico; we stole it from the gachupines (the men with spurs), whose ties were with our mother country, Spain. This priest Hidalgo and his horde of mestizos who began this revolution do not have the intelligence to run Mexico. It was left up to us to make sure the revolution succeeded and we replaced the gachupines at the top of the social scale. The station in life of the mestizos is far below that of ours. The union of lonely Spanish soldiers with Indian women early in our history, produced these inbred peons. They are the ones who have made a crack in our social structure. We must eradicate this crack before it widens. Otherwise it will trip us and we will fall into that crack and be forgotten for many years to come."

"What about the Indians?" Gallegos mused.

"The Christianized Indians can be controlled by our ally, the Church, the unchristianized Indians on the frontier can be controlled by the army." The major hesitated for a moment, "Our concern right now is with this Benito Juarez fellow. It is difficult for me to believe that he has the intelligence to lead the mestizos. Perhaps he is one of those unexplained phenomenon which happen every so often.

"What we need now for our country is a strong leader who will bring stability and continuity of leadership. After Iturbides' leadership ended you remember, we went through a period of time in which we had one president after another. Santa Anna, himself, took the office of the presidency six times. It is imperative, it seems to me, that what we must do first is to elect a president who is strong and who is willing to use whatever force is required to maintain stability."

"I agree with you entirely, Major, and I also contend that such leadership can come only through the aristocratic class. Can you imagine what would happen if the mestizos gained control of our presidency and placed uneducated peons in places of authority? Whose only criterion to hold office is that they come from the mestizo class? The country would be in chaos immediately, thus inviting other countries to come in and dismember us again.''

''No, we must not allow this to happen,'' the major replied. ''We must stop this Juarez fellow before he destroys Mexico. We now have a government in Mexico City which is to our liking, but at the same time, this Benito Juarez Indian claims to head the official government, the only difference being that his government is on the run. President Miramon rules in Mexico City and has appealed to and received help from some European countries.

''Juarez, on the other hand, has asked for and received help from the gringo Americanos. It seems Juarez tries to run his country from Washington, D.C. In fact I overheard someone say in Chihuahua the other day that his headquarters is in Washington.''

This major likes to talk, thought Gallegos as he looked at his pocket watch. ''Tomorrow will be a busy day, Major, so perhaps we should get a good night's sleep.''

''You are correct, my friend,'' the major slapped both knees with the palms of his hands and rose, ''I want to find those Apaches as soon as possible and be on my way. There is much need for soldiers these days,'' he said complacently.

After entering his room, the major carefully locked his door. As he lit a match to light the lamp, he heard a movement behind him and with the match held high, he turned and looked into the eyes of Crazy Legs and Great Star, again dressed in their Apache attire. That was the last he saw before he was struck unconscious. They then painted a yellow stripe under each of his eyes and carried him quietly to the head of the stairs and let his limp form roll down them. After several revolutions, the major came to a rest face up and as he regained consciousness, he moaned. Damacio was the first to hear, and he called to the patron as he ran to the major.

Gallegos came running with a lamp in one hand and a pistol in the other. He looked down at Romero with a horrified expression.

''The Apaches were here again!''

''How did you know that?'' The major wavered as he attempted to rise.

''Look in that mirror down the hall and see for yourself,'' his host answered shortly.

When the major walked unsteadily to the mirror and peered at himself, he whipped out his handkerchief and dabbed at the stripes, trying angrily to erase the yellow paint. "I'm beginning to understand your problem, Gallegos. They were Apaches; I saw them with my own eyes. Peons could not pose as those Apaches," he spoke softly to himself.

"Are you all right, Luis?" Gallegos asked.

"Yes, the only thing really hurt is my pride," came the major's reply. "Could you bring me a double shot of whiskey, Damacio?"

"Pronto," Gallegos urged.

The two men entered the major's bedroom and Gallegos began to search it.

"They are gone, Gallegos, so stop searching. You don't think they would be stupid enough to stick around after what they did to me, do you?"

Damacio entered the room at that moment with the whiskey, preventing a sharp retort from the patron. He nodded curtly and left the room with Damacio as the major drank the whiskey and then once more began to retire for the night. Turning out the lamp, he crawled gratefully into bed. He lay there looking at the ceiling, trying to devise a plan whereby he could snare the Apache devils. Intermittently, the moon cast light into the room as the clouds passed in front of it. A feeling of danger nearby came over the major and his eyes went quickly to the window. There stood the outlines of two Apaches, no doubt the same who had visited him earlier. He threw the bedclothes to one side and cursed not having his pistol at hand. By the time he reached it and again turned toward the window the figures were no longer there. He opened the window and peered out cautiously, nothing, he then stepped out onto the balcony which ran the length of the side of the house, still nothing, all was still as his eyes searched the darkness. He finally returned once more to his room, locking the window, and again lay down, this time with his pistol on the quilt beside him. His eyes closed and he dozed off, then fell into a deep sleep. A scratching on the window awakened him and before he had even opened his eyes, his hand searched for the pistol. Finding it, he swiftly turned toward the window and fired four consecutive shots. The window was shattered, but when he rushed to look out, once more there was nothing to be seen.

Loud knocking on his door, and the sound of voices interrupted him and he rushed to unlock the door. Gallegos rushed into the room, pistol in hand. "Apaches again?"

"Damn them," the major cursed in reply, "they have more

audacity than any I've ever seen, in a people known for their share of it.''

"I'll post two guards outside your windows for the remainder of the night," the patron said firmly.

"I hate to admit it, but I'm afraid you'd better," the major conceded. Damacio was sent to tell Miguel to post two guards, immediately.

When the guards presented themselves,the major stepped through his window to inspect them. "What are your names?"

"Fermin and Ramon Salas," was their reply.

"Be alert!" The major was stern of face and manner. "These Apaches are clever. If you see or hear anything suspicious, call me immediately. Do you understand?" He turned back to his room feeling more secrure with two guards stationed outside. When the major had shut his window and pulled the curtain, a small smile could have been seen on each of the faces of his guards.

At daylight, the major and his troops were saddling up, preparing to ride out, when a rider was seen riding at a gallop toward the barns. He was yelling, but was too far out as yet to be heard. He waved his sombrero and continued to approach at breakneck speed.

"He is yelling, 'Apaches', senor," Miguel told the major.

"Apaches!" The major brightened, "So that's where those two of last night went. Dese prisa (hurry up) muchachos, we are going to catch those treacherous, yellow faced devils and put an end to their foolishness for all time!"

The rider pulled in his grateful, sweat-stained horse in front of the patron, swept off his sombrero, and gasped, "Apaches are stealing the horses, senor. They have killed Vicente and Porfiro, and have the others pinned down at the stone line camp. Without help, they will not last."

"How many Apaches are there?" Gallegos asked.

"Maybe ten or twelve," came the reply from the worn out rider. "Please, senor, they are running low on ammunition."

"Mount up, men! Gallegos, we'll be back with your Apache ghosts muy pronto."

"Why don't you take some of my men with you? They know right where the stone line camp is and they could be of some help to you."

"All right, but tell them to hurry. I don't want those devils to get away."

Miguel yelled at Crazy Legs and Great Star to saddle up and

several others also went for their horses. Within five minutes, they were riding at a fast lope for the line camp, Miguel, Great Star, and Crazy Legs in the lead. After half an hour of hard riding, they began to hear gunfire in the distance. As they reached the knoll of a small hill, they could see below them, at a distance of perhaps half a mile, the vaqueros defending themselves against the Indians. As they drew nearer, one by one the Apaches moved back, jumped on their horses and withdrew, racing toward the west.

Miguel, Crazy Legs, and Great Star rode toward the vaqueros while the soldiers rode after the Apaches. After seeing that the vaqueros were safe, Crazy Legs and Great Star jumped into their saddles, and Miguel asked where they were going. "To help the soldiers," Crazy Legs told him. They spurred their horses as he spoke, kicking dirt into Miguel's face as they rushed to catch up with the soldiers.

"Not me!" Miguel yelled after them. "Let the soldiers do that job. I'll not risk my neck when I don't have to."

The other vaqueros heartily agreed with Miguel's philosophy, for they'd had enough of the Apaches for one day.

Meanwhile, Crazy Legs and Great Star hurried to get into the fight, though it is doubtful that the major was looking for their brand of help. They heard gunshots off to their left, and they came within sight of the soldiers firing toward a brushy canyon. They couldn't see their quarry, but assumed that the soldiers were able to see them. They dismounted and hid their horses, tying them securely, then pulled red headbands from inside their shirts and fastened them across their foreheads.

"Our brethren won't shoot at us now," Crazy Legs grinned. He checked his rifle and began to walk in a crouched position toward the soldiers. Great Star followed, moving cautiously, but swiftly. They had approached within a few hundred yards of the soldiers before they camouflaged themselves with the vegetation. When they had finished and were ready to move on, they could hardly see each other.

A few minutes later, Great Star said, I'll take the major." He aimed his rifle, took a deep breath and squeezed the trigger. Major Romero fell face downward and didn't move. Almost at the same moment his lieutenant fell, hit by Crazy Legs. Upon seeing the officers fall, the Mexican sergeant took command.

"Do you think the sergeant is smart enough to leave, or do you think he'll be foolish enough to continue the fight?" Great Star wondered aloud.

"Let's help him to make up his mind," Crazy Legs answered. He aimed his rifle and another soldier fell.

"Have you spotted the sergeant yet?" Great Star asked as he fired once more.

"Four down and sixteen to go," said Crazy Legs, grimly.

"We don't know how many have been killed by our brothers," Great Star pointed out.

"How many can you count that are down? I count seven," said Crazy Legs.

"I count eight," said his brother as he made a good shot.

"The important thing is whether the ones who are left are anxious to continue with this," Crazy Legs commented, "they don't seem to be letting up any."

Before they fired another shot, one more of the soldiers toppled over. As he did, they saw the remaining soldiers fall back and then run for their mounts. They soon disappeared to the south.

It was too quiet for a few minutes and then a voice called, "Identify yourselves."

"Mescaleros." Great Star responded.

When that word reached the others, they began to rise from behind boulders and bushy vegetation and walk toward the two brothers who had also risen. The others were Lipan Apaches, whose chief spoke to them in Spanish, for their language was not familiar to the Lipans. The chief was resplendent in his attire. He wore a rosary around his neck, a prize from some unfortunate Mexican victim, probably. He wore an animal skin fur hat through which was stuck an eagle feather. The others wore typical Lipan clothing, with many of them also wearing an article taken from some Mexican who had unfortunately come into contact with them. Some wore Christian crosses around their necks, while others wore Mexican belts and still others rode Mexican saddles. A few even wore the medals which some dead Mexican soldiers had won for bravery, or for performing some act above and beyond the call of duty for the ordinary soldier.

"My Mexican name is Jose," the leader of the little band said.

Crazy Legs and Great Star introduced themselves and the Mescaleros did not insult the Lipan leader by asking his Apache name which is very personal, for very special occasions, only.

After some discussion, the Mescaleros told the Lipans of their mission in Mexico. While they were talking, some of the others rode over to the scattered dead soldiers and stripped them of whatever of value they carried or wore. When they returned, they were apprised of the plan which their leader and the Mescaleros had worked out. Together, they were going to steal all of the horses on the hacienda, both the ones out on pasture and the prize ones in the stables. To accomplish this feat, it was decided that the Apaches would pair off into five parties, each party consisting of three braves.

Crazy Legs and Great Star were to lure Gallegos out to the herd with the ostensible purpose of burying the major and his men who had fallen in battle. While Gallegos was having this done, the Lipans would attack him and his burial party. Crazy Legs and Great Star would then volunteer for the dangerous job of getting through the line of attackers and riding to the hacienda for help.

When the Mescaleros and the Lipans had the plans worked out to their satisfaction, Crazy Legs and Great Star rode back to the headquarters. When they were within two miles of their destination, they spurred their horses into a run, and pulled them in, breathing hard, in front of the big house.

"Patron . . . patron!" They yelled without dismounting.

Gallegos rushed out of the front door and onto the verandah.

"What's wrong?"

"Major Romero is dead, patron, and so are some of his soldiers," Crazy Legs gasped.

"What of the battle? Who won? Were the Apaches killed?" Gallegos shot the questions at the two vaqueros.

"When the soldiers, Miguel, Ramon and I and the others reached the horse herd, the Apaches broke off the attack and retreated, and Major Romero gave orders to pursue the Apaches and Ramon and I went with them. Miguel remained with the others to watch the horse herd. There was a battle in which the major, his lieutenant and some of his soldiers were killed. When the soldiers realized that their officers had been killed, they retreated toward Chihuahua, leaving the dead soldiers to be plundered by the Apaches. When the soldiers left the field of battle, Ramon and I rode as fast as we could to tell you of what happened."

"What about the Apaches? Did they also leave?"

"The last we saw of them, patron, they were racing for the Sierra Madres, carrying their dead and wounded with them. The major fought bravely, and before he fell he killed at least six Apaches in singlehanded combat. I don't think the Apaches will ever come again to this hacienda. They paid too dear a price and left emptyhanded," he concluded.

"Tell the patron about how the major fought the Apache chief

119

in hand-to-hand combat, Fermin!''

''Hand-to-hand combat?'' Gallegos questioned.

''Si, it was the killing of the Apache chief which made his braves finally flee. On seeing the major, the Apache chief seemed to go crazy. He rushed at the major, waving a knife and when his horse reached the major, the chief jumped at him and they both hit the ground. The major lost his pistol, but the Apache still had his knife. Seeing that the major was defenseless, the Apache rushed him once more. The major grabbed the hand which held the knife and raised his leg, smashing the Apache's arm on his knee. The Apache dropped the knife, and the major kicked him in the groin with his boot. When the chief doubled over, the major picked up the knife and plunged it into the Apache's back. Upon seeing their chief fall, three Apaches made a move to retrieve the body of their leader. One of them shot the major, but my brother, here, killed two of them. The third threw the body of the dead chief across his horse and galloped off. I think I may have hit him, for he straightened suddenly, but if he died later from the wound, I don't know. Once the body of their chief had been retrieved, the rest of the Apaches followed.''

Crazy Legs glanced at his brother, then back at the patron, saying earnestly, ''That major was the bravest man I ever saw, and he was not afraid of those Apaches; if anything they were afraid of him. He seemed anxious to tangle with them. That was one brave hombre. Mexico will miss him.''

''We lost the major, it is true,'' the patron spoke matter-of-factly, ''but he accomplished his mission; he got rid of those Apache dogs. He was a good soldier and a pride to his country. He showed a rare kind of courage, and courage which will be emulated by others of his breed in the trying days and months ahead. With such brave men as Major Luis Romero, Mexico's destiny is secured.''

''Patron,'' Great Star said, ''we cannot leave that brave man's body out there for the vultures to pick apart. He must be buried with the highest honors which his country can give him. That is the least we can do for him.''

''You are right, Ramon, get a buckboard and saddle a horse for me. We will bring the major back to the house.''

Crazy Legs drove the buckboard, his horse tied to the back of it, and Gallegos and Great Star rode in the lead. All was calm when they reached Miguel and the vaqueros.

''Come with me,'' Gallegos ordered, ''we are going for the

bodies of our countrymen."

The vaqueros mounted and formed a double line behind the buckboard. When they reached the dead soldiers, the Lipans opened fire from all directions.

"We are surrounded," Miguel shouted as he leaped from his saddle, pulling his rifle from its scabbard. "Take cover, muchachos!"

The Apaches kept up a continuous fire at the pinned down Mexicans, and Gallegos turned to Crazy Legs accusingly, "I thought you told me that they had retreated toward the Sierra Madres."

"They did retreat toward the Sierra Madres."

"Then who are they?" Gallegos pointed a finger at empty space in anger.

"Patron, I swear that they ran for the mountains. I saw them."

"We'll talk about that later; right now we have to get out of here. What do you think we should do, Miguel?"

Miguel raised his head slowly, but pulled it down quickly, as a bullet whistled past. "We need help . . . there are too many of them out there for such a small number as we are," he told his patron.

"It would be suicide for anyone to try to ride for help. He would be cut down before he took two steps." Gallegos looked about him to see if any of his men had been hit as yet.

"Two might make it," Crazy Legs suggested.

"Two? How could two make it easier than one?"

"Ramon and I could crawl over to the horses and fasten our belts around their necks. We could hold on to the belts with our hands and place our toes over the rumps of the horses. I could ride on the left horse on the right side and Ramon do just the opposite so we would be sandwiched in between the horses. We could run a rope between them to keep them together as they run. In that way we would be invisible except from the front or back."

"It's a crazy idea, but it might work," Miguel commented.

"What other choices do we have? Do it, and if you get through I'll never forget you, and if you don't get through, we'll all meet in heaven or hell!" Gallegos told them.

The horses were tied together, and Crazy Legs and Great Star positioned themselves between them, and with one swift slap on the rumps by Miguel and Gallegos, they sprang on their way. Miguel, and the patron and the others held their breaths as they watched the two horses dash off in the direction of the ranch headquarters. No one moved or spoke, for all knew that their best hope of getting out of this predicament depended upon the two men who were taking such risks.

"I don't like this stillness," Gallegos finally muttered, "why have the Apaches stopped firing? Do they suspect what we have done?"

"We'll see in a few seconds," Miguel said as he kept his eyes on the running horses.

Suddenly, two Apaches appeared out of nowhere and made a grab for the running horses. One was pushed to one side by a horse's shoulder, but the other succeeded in jumping to the back of the other horse, but within seconds he, too, tumbled to the ground.

"I think they're going to make it," Gallegos said with satisfaction.

Crazy Legs and Great Star could be seen pulling themselves upright on their horses' backs and untying the rope which held them together, all of this happening as they continued to gallop toward the headquarters.

Gallegos and the men now saw two Apaches ride from behind the boulders to give chase.

"God, I hope they make it!" Gallegos breathed.

The Lipans took up their shooting again, keeping the Mexicans pinned down.

When Crazy Legs and Great Star had ridden out of sight of the besieged men, they pulled in their horses to wait for the two Lipans to come up with them.

"Just before we reach headquarters, you two will hide in the brush or wherever you'll be out of sight, until the rest of the peons leave to support the patron. Once they have left, you move in to drive the horses northward until you rendezvous with the others who'll have the rest of the horses. Great Star and I will finish our work here and join you on the trail or at your village. We'll take our share of the horses and head for the Sierra Blancas. Any questions?"

The Lipans shook their heads, grinned, and began to look for a suitable place to conceal themselves while the two brothers rode on to the ranch buildings.

All was peaceful there and the peons went about their work unaware of what was happening on another part of the hacienda. Suddenly the peal of the church bell rang out to warn them of some emergency or danger. They quickly assembled in front of the patron's big house, some of them rushing to their cottages first to make sure their families had also heard the summons. When they had all gathered, Crazy Legs and Great Star told them of what had happened and asked the men to ready themselves to ride to help the patron and the men with him.

There was a hesitation and all eyes turned to Placido, who moved past his workers and walked up onto the steps leading to the patio gate. "We are followers of Benito Juarez. Why should we save that creole and Miguel?"

There were murmurs of agreement from the rest.

"So you're the one," Crazy Legs said as he looked at Placido approvingly, "we knew that someone was the leader of the Juarez people here on the hacienda. We suspected that it might be you, but we did not know for sure. Is everyone with you? Are Damacio and Juana also supporters of Juarez?"

"All here now at the hacienda are with me, with the exception of the wife of the patron, and as of this moment she is our prisoner!" Placido declared proudly. "But what about you two? I've kept my eye on you, for you have puzzled me. Sometimes I've thought you were on our side, and sometimes that you were spies?"

"Spies? For whom, the Federales?" Crazy Legs laughed.

"If you're not a creole supporter and you are not for Benito Juarez, who are you?"

Crazy Legs glanced at his brother, and his brother nodded. "We are Apaches from the Sierra Blanca mountains far north of here."

Murmurs could be heard from the peons once more, this time in fright and nervousness, and they shrank backward.

"If you don't care what happens to Gallegos and Miguel, what about the vaqueros? Aren't they with you? Will you let them be killed?"

Placido didn't answer immediately, but looked at the two brothers and then asked one more question, "Why are you here?"

Crazy Legs and Great Star then spoke of Magdalena and told of what Gallegos had done to some of her people.

"Why haven't you done something to Gallegos, then?"

"We have been, and we will do more today," Great Star answered.

"What we would like for you to do," Crazy Legs told him, "is to go to rescue Gallegos. The Apaches who have them pinned down are with us. When they see you coming, they will retreat, taking the horse herd with them. My brother and I had planned to take these prize horses here and join the Apaches later, but I guess we'll have to change our plans a little."

"How?" Placido was interested.

"Great Star," said his brother, "tell one of the Apaches hiding just outside to take a message to Jose. Ask him to tell Jose to kill the two men who lead the vaqueros, but to allow the vaqueros with them to return to the headquarters."

As Great Star left on his errand, Crazy Legs turned back to Placido, saying, "You heard what I told my brother. It is your responsibility to make sure that your people ride well behind Miguel and the patron. They must continue to ride toward home after the two have been killed, however.

"Now take your men and go to the rescue of the patron! One thing more, remember that we are Apaches and understand deceit and treachery. We didn't have to play Apache as Major Romero thought some of your people had been doing. My brother and I were those Apaches. Do you understand my meaning?"

"Si," Placido replied grimly. He turned to order Damacio to give all of the weapons available in the big house to his men. "The rest of you take knives, pitch forks, or anything else which can be used as a weapon. Remember, once we reach where Gallegos is, the Apaches will not shoot at you, but only near you. We must convince Gallegos and Miguel that we've risked our lives to save them. Then stay well in the rear as Miguel and the patron lead us back to the house, or you could be shot by mistake. Savvy?"

A chorus of voices assured him of their understanding.

"Then let's get our horses and weapons and ride."

Within two hours, Miguel and the patron were dead, the Apaches were departing with the prize horses and Placido and his peons were once more at headquarters. Mrs. Gallegos would be allowed to go to Chihuahua unharmed, for Juana wanted it to be that way.

That same night, in the far reaches of the hacienda, Crazy Legs, Great Star and the Lipans stayed late around their campfire. They discussed changes in the world around them, and their concern for the future of the Indian way of life and its approaching end.

"Are we to follow the great Aztec civilization into extinction? Will we become as they are now, a mixture of other races?" These things Jose wondered aloud.

Great Star answered, "My brother and I are products of mixed races. Are we different from you in any way? We were raised as Apaches and we believe that we are one hundred per cent Apache, but there is a difference between us and what is happening in Mexico. We were raised by Apaches, in an Apache environment. There is no single environment in America or in Mexico. They are still in the process of making their own culture. The Apache will contribute to this new culture. What is important in this coming together of different cultures is justice and equality. If everyone is treated and accepted as an equal, and justice is observed, it might work. But that is not happening in Mexico yet. People like Gallegos run everything and for one not of his class, there is no justice or equality.

"The Aztecs developed a great civilization, but look at them now. Most sleep on straw mats and their main diet is beans and corn. They once built beautiful stone temples which reached the sky, but now they live in dirt shacks. Those who married the Spaniards raised a new breed of Mexicans called mestizos, part Indian and part Spanish, and as mestizo married mestizo, this class grew, but was not accepted as equal to the creoles. The peons here on this hacienda are of the mestizos. All they have lacked is a leader, and now I think he has arrived."

"Who is he?" Jose asked.

"An Indian who calls himself Benito Juarez. He is not a mestizo, but a Zapotec Indian, but he speaks for all Mexicans. He was very young when his parents died so he was left with his uncle. When the revolution of independence from Spain began, Benito was a shepherd boy. Dissatisfied with this, he ran away and was later helped to get an education by someone who adopted him. He considered the priesthood, but decided that this was not for him. And now he has risen all the way to the presidency of Mexico . . . at least president of some of the people. He is not recognized by people such as Gallegos," Crazy Legs concluded.

Just then it was reported that one of the lookouts had spotted Mexican soldiers camped ten to fifteen miles south of the hacienda headquarters. It was thought that some of them may have been with the major but had now joined with another force. There were approximately thirty-five soldiers in all. Jose looked at Crazy Legs and Great Star and offered to follow their lead.

"But these braves are your followers; they look to you for leadership. My brother and I are only two and we are Mescaleros, not Lipans. We will follow your leadership," Crazy Legs said.

"We are all Apaches now, we are not Mescaleros or Lipans. It is my wish that you lead. My leadership has not been tested as strongly as yours and your brother's. I will tell my braves to listen only to you," Jose spoke with finality.

Crazy Legs ordered four Lipans to continue driving the horse herd toward the Sierra Madres. "The rest of us will stay behind to delay, or if possible, destroy the soldiers."

"Sergeant Montoya," Captain Sanchez called. The sun had not yet peeped over the ridge to the east of the camp, but the sergeant presented himself promptly before his captain and saluted.

"Prepare the men to move out, Sergeant, and no bugle calls, we don't want to alert the Apaches."

"Si, my captain," Montoya responded with a snappy salute.

Shortly thereafter, the Mexican soldiers moved out of camp in a column of two's, the captain and the sergeant leading them.

"Sergeant," the captain said in a low voice, "ride back along the column and remind the men to be as quiet as possible, and to keep their eyes and ears alert for Indian sign. We have with us some of the best Indian fighters in the states of Chihuahua and Sonora, so they know what we're looking for. With these men we will destroy the dogs who killed my friend, Major Luis Romero. When I get my hands on them, they'll wish they'd never entered Mexico!"

The soldier behind the captain spoke softly, "Apaches, captain, to your right. He pointed to a lone Apache who sat his pony on a nearby hill. "A scout would be my guess."

"Yes, Florencio, I think you're right. It is difficult to hide from Apaches. They seem to know every move we make, and sometimes I think they can smell an enemy ten miles away! Well, we know for sure that they realize we're after them."

The Mexican column continued, following the trail of the stolen horses and keeping track of the scout who kept pace with them in the distance. On their second day out, rain destroyed the tracks and the captain ordered five of his best men to scatter to try to pick up new tracks. Florencio was one of the five men who searched for new sign. He spurred his horse into a lope in the direction of the lone Apache, checking his pistols as he rode. He pulled his knife from its scabbard and then pushed it back in. He chewed on

126

some tobacco, spitting to his left now and then. He noticed that the Apache scout pulled back behind the hill as he approached. He studied the ground as he rode, watching for any sign of disturbance, and he listened for any sound which could warn of danger. As he cautiously rode up the hill where he'd seen the Apache, his horse's ears pricked up and looking in that direction, he saw probably the same scout sitting on a ridge perhaps a quarter of a mile away. Florencio kept an eye on him as he rode in that direction, and recognized him as a Lipan. The only movement visible was the westerly wind blowing the tail of the pony. Most Lipans dressed similarly to the Comanches and wore long braids. They also wore leather clothing with colorful beadwork as did the Comanches. Florencio sat his horse for a few seconds, his rifle resting on his lap, as he studied the Apache. The Apache returned his stare as he also sat, still as a statue, watching the soldier. After a few minutes of this silent scrutiny, the scout reined his pony away once more and disappeared behind the ridge.

Florencio sat wondering if the Apache were trying to lure him into a trap. After debating with himself, he decided to ride back to the column, where he reported that while he had not found any new trace of the stolen horses, he had seen the Apache close up, close enough to identify his tribe. When the other four who had been detailed to look for tracks returned, they too, had had no luck.

Crazy Legs had sent his braves out in different directions to try to lure the Mexican column into giving chase, thus giving the horseherders a bigger lead, and time to reach the Sierra Madres. The rain had conspired to help them elude the soldiers, for the soldiers hadn't picked up the trail again.

Captain Sanchez, being the experienced Indian fighter that he was, suspected a trap and determined to keep his main body of men together while they searched for fresh tracks. He decided to ride due north, believing that if he were on the right scent, the Apaches would attempt to harass them, while if they were on a false scent, they'd be left alone. After remaining on this tack for several miles with no further sign of Apaches, the captain ordered a new direction, due west. He reasoned that the Apaches would either make a run for their homeland, which was in the north, or they would make for the Sierra Madres and their many hiding places, which were west of their present position. Once concealed in the mountains, they could wait until he and his men tired of the search and went home. The more he considered this possibility, the more convinced he became that the herd was being driven westward. The rest of the day passed without any further sighting of either the tracks they sought or of Indian scouts, but the captain was convinced that they were on the right trail, and he pressed on in that direction. They made camp about sundown and he told his men to be ready to ride at sunup.

The next day, the Mexican troopers led by Captain Sanchez rode over one series of hills after another until they reached a long stretch of relatively flat country. A number of dry arroyos were scattered throughout this area. From one of these arroyos, the Apaches opened fire without warning upon their enemy, killing or wounding at least six soldiers. After the Apaches had fired their rifles to such good advantage, they slid down the side of the deep arroyo, mounted their ponies, and galloped down the winding gulch, leaving the Mexicans to proceed cautiously to see if they all had left. Upon reaching the rim and seeing that only empty rifle shells and pony tracks remained, the captain realized that his mission was a dismal failure. Not only had he gotten some of his men killed and others wounded, but they were now in the foothills of the Sierra Madres, the sanctuary of many Apache bands. It would be insane to enter these mountains any farther and expose his men to any further depredations.

High above the soldiers, Crazy Legs and Great Star and Jose, the Lipan chief, watched as the Mexican soldiers tended their wounded, buried two men and slowly rode down off the plateau and away.

Crazy Legs turned to Jose and said, "If my brother and I take eight horses of our choice from the herd, would there be any objections from our brothers, the Lipans?"

Jose tuned in his saddle to face the Mescalero and answered, "Take as many as you want and which ones you want; after all if it were not for you two, we Lipans would be fewer and maybe none at all, but because of you we are here and have horses also."

"Eight of our choice would be all that we would want. Any more than that would draw too much attention and make it more difficult to reach our destination safely," Crazy Legs smiled, "it would be better to travel with fewer horses and get there than travel with too many and not reach there at all."

"The Mescalero speaks with wisdom," answered Jose, "take the horses of your choice with my blessing and may Usen guide and protect you on your journey to a reunion with your people. We will speak of you with fondness and pride when we gather around our campfires this winter."

The Mescaleros cut out the horses of their choice from the herd and placed horsehair halters on them. As they rode away, they were each leading four of the finest horses they'd ever seen, as a present for their father, Thunderbolt.

"Why don't we travel northeastward and make our way home by passing between Fort Bliss at El Paso and Fort Hancock on the Rio Grande further south? After we have these forts to our backs, we can then turn northward, keeping the Guadalupes to the east until we reach the Sacramentos. We can travel up the western slope of those mountains until we reach Dog Canyon up which we can ride until we reach the high country of our stronghold," suggested Crazy Legs.

There was much excitement as the two rode into the camp high in the Sierra Blancas. Young boys were lined up as usual to take the horses. Evening Star and Thunderbolt stood in front of their tepee waiting to greet them as their sons walked in their direction. All four entered their tepee and Evening Star directed her sons to sit on some newly tanned buffalo robes, while she prepared food for them. "We want to hear where you've been and what you have done before you go to the ceremony to tell all of the others," their mother said with obvious pride in her voice.

The two men told their parents of their adventures, which they repeated later to all of the people at the ceremony honoring them and their achievements. Evening Star thanked her sons for the fine gingham cloth which they had sent to her by way of the other Apache warriors after the killing of the Mexican soldiers near Chupadera Flats.

Thunderbolt told his sons that the mules and horses had also been delivered in good shape. When Crazy Legs and Great Star had finished relating their adventures, they asked their parents to tell them what had happened in their absence."

"Much has happened, and none of it good," Thunderbolt told his sons. "While you were gone, the big war between the white eyes began far to the east of here, in the land of your mother. This war needs many warriors, so most of the forts here have been reduced in strength. This weakness encouraged many Apaches and others to step up their raids in hopes of driving the white eyes out of our country once and for all.

"Ranches, villages, sheepherders, soldiers, forts, all were being attacked on a regular basis by Apaches, Comanches and Navajos. Many white eyes were killed and others did not always replace them, but this was not true with the soldiers. There always seemed to be more to replace them. It's as though their number were inexhaustable. From what you have told us this evening, this is true, though most of us can't comprehend such numbers.

"One side of the white eyes army wears blue uniforms and the other side wears gray. The gray side took Fort Bliss away from the blue warriors. They then marched up the Rio Grande and took the forts of the blue warriors as they marched. The soldiers at Fort Stanton fled without giving a fight, but destroyed the fort before they left. The gray warrior soldiers occupied it for awhile, but later abandoned it, because of a heavy, constant attack by our people. Kit Carson then came with his New Mexico soldiers and rebuilt the fort. The gray soldiers were defeated badly up north and retreated back down into Texas. All of this is bad news for us, but what appears to be the worst news of all is that a column of soldiers which left California to help drive the gray warriors back into Texas, arrived too late for the fight, so what they're doing now is fighting all Indians. They are talking of putting us into cages which they call reservations. The chief of these California soldiers is called Carleton. He is a mean one, this one is, he ordered all Apaches killed on sight, even if we should wish to surrender. Do not try to surrender my sons, because if you try, even if you use a white flag, the soldiers will shoot you down. That is how things stand now, as of today."

Crazy Legs turned to his mother and said, "I remember when you told us that this day would come. Great Star and I have traveled to Santa Fe, Las Vegas, and then down into Mexico. That country has many problems which will take her many years to solve. But here in America it is quite different. The Mexicans are fighting among themselves, but that is not true of the Americans, except for this new war. They are unified and aggressive; they are full of ambition, and they have a vision of what they want their country to become. They face danger without fear; they are eager to get on with their country's destiny. I do not think they can be stopped. The Indians are only one of the obstacles which will either have to throw in with them or be pushed aside. Our future, as you once said, Mother, is bleak and it is here now, at our door.

"We do not have many options to survive, whereas the Americans have numerous options, many of which will eventually bring them success. The way I see it, is that we can resist the American encroachment until we are mostly destroyed, or we can deal with them and hope that enough of us survive to keep our culture alive. At least in this second option, our dead will be remembered, out culture could be preserved, and our history remembered. I have spoken. What are the thoughts of my parents and brother?''

It was quiet for long moments as each gazed into the fire. It was Thunderbolt who finally broke the stillness, "We must call for a council meeting and present these views before the people and then permit others to give their views. That is the law. I believe your mother and brother both agree with your position. Is that not so?'' Thunderbolt rose to his feet and looked down at his wife and younger son.

A council meeting was called a short time later, and when it was time, Crazy Legs and his brother, Great Star told of what they had seen and what they had concluded from their findings. Crazy Legs looked around the circle of his people for a few seconds without speaking. Then he began, "It is difficult for me to say what I feel I must say now. What I am about to say to you will not be easy for any of you to hear, or for me to say, but it must be said, and you must respond. Time requires that I say what I am about to say and time requires that you give your thoughts.

"We are called the People, Dine, Inde, and Apache. We are Usen's chosen people. No one is superior to our people, no one can equal us in warfare; no one can equal us in bravery, honor, or discipline. We stand alone, we stand apart from all others. We are a proud people and a loyal people; there will always be Mescaleros. Our spirit will haunt our land for eternity, and our souls will never miss a day of earthly life. Usen will never forget our devotion to him. He, in His own time and His own way, will again place us in charge of our destiny. If we continue to believe in him, he will continue to guide us. He will never forget the Apache. But now, my fellow Apaches, hard times have befallen us, and our first thought must be for our survival. We must think of our children and their children; we must find a way to survive as part of this new nation that spreads westward as does a prairie fire. This westward movement of the Americans has just begun; more will come, many more, so many that they will number as many as the trees on Sierra Blanca and more. They will fall upon us as snowflakes; we must find a way to survive as part of this new nation called America, and at the same time find a way to preserve our ways. I have spoken from the heart of an Apache; I have spoken from the mind of an Apache; I have spoken from my soul; I have spoken."

He looked toward his mother. "Now my mother wishes to speak," he said proudly.

"I am an Apache woman," Evening Star said, "I belong to a tribe which permits their women to speak with no fear of reprisal from their braves. That cannot be said of many nations, whether it be Indian, Mexican, or American. Apache women may, if they so choose, even accompany Apache men on raids. Their council is listened to at the council meetings. We are a free people, with equality provided for all, but I also remember my childhood days which were spent with Americans. I know America. It has a good heart; it too, has justice and equality.

"I believe that we have three choices and not two, as you have said, my son. Added to your two is the third option of migrating into the Sierra Madre mountains of Mexico. There, we can continue our ways for many years, but the day will come there, also, as it has come here, when we will have just the two options which you have put forth. Today, now, we have the option of becoming Americans and if we migrate to Mexico, we will eventually face what we face now, the only difference being that we will not have the option of becoming Americans; we will have to become Mexicans. I say America."

Next, Standing Bear rose to speak and he spoke angrily, "Most of the young braves oppose joining the Americans, we say that surrender is for cowards and women. If we surrender, we will be laughed at and made fun of by these Americans. We will be spat upon and insulted. Too many years will be required to pass before we will be accepted as equals by the Americans. I will be in the sky world many years before that happens. I say we fight; it is better to fight and die as Apaches rather than surrender to the Americans and become of them."

Standing Bear led a small group of braves, not as many as he had hoped for, from the council meeting and disappeared into the darkness . . . they would become the nucleus of another outlaw band of Apaches who would make war upon all white eyes, raids which would bring punishment upon peaceful Apaches by the soldiers and Indian agents. Most white men would not take the time to try to understand that the Apache nation had outlaws just as did their society.

CHAPTER FOURTEEN

Many of the small villages along the Rio Grande were hit by the flood of 1862, for they had been built too close to the lifeblood of the people of the Rio Grande Valley. The river broke its banks everywhere, bringing with it destruction, disease and death. The muddy water inched its way further and further across the fertile, green fields toward the homes and barns, and finally into the streets. The water slowly eroded the adobe walls of all buildings as it deepened, until the walls could no longer stand. Collapsing walls disappeared as the rushing water continued on its destructive rampage. Those who had some warning of the approaching high water were able to salvage something, but most only had time to save themselves.

One by one, family by family, the disheartened people made their way toward Mesilla. Some walked, some rode burros or horseback, the lucky ones carried their personal belongings in carretas. The long lines of dejected, lost souls trudged wearily and in their faces could be seen disappointment, but not despair, for these were the children of those courageous conquistadores who had conquered nations for Spain. This would be another setback in a long line of setbacks, for disaster was no stranger to these hardy, pioneer people.

For hundreds of years, ever since their ancestors had come to the shores of this new land, disaster after disaster had befallen them, but time after time these people gathered what belongings they could salvage and began anew, gaining from each disaster, lessons which built into them stamina, character, endurance, and self reliance. It seemed that each new generation grew stronger and more understanding of the elements.

At Mesilla, they built shelters for protection against the hot sun which beat down upon the open, rolling, semi-desert land high above the destructive reach of the waters of the river. The people of Mesilla opened their village, hearts, and homes to their unfortunate compadres. They made sure that no one went hungry or lacked what was necessary for survival. After many meetings and much discussion, some of the flood victims decided to chance settling near the mouth of the Tularosa River which though not far from the Mescalero stronghold in the Sierra Blanca mountains above the Tularosa, would provide the so vital water for them to survive.

Thus it was that one cold November morning, before dawn, a

column of carretas pulled by plodding oxen and laden with farm equipment, tools, and seed, moved slowly up the slope toward the San Augustin Pass. Some men walked along beside their carretas with a bullwhip which they used to keep their oxen moving. Others rode horseback. Scouts rode ahead, behind, and on both flanks to warn of danger. Only ten to fifteen miles could be traveled each day because of the slow pace of the oxen.

Their first night was spent on San Augustin Pass, below which could be seen fifty miles of comparatively flat terrain. A sea of grass, belly high to a horse, could be seen bending eastward before the soft western wind. The scouts looked down upon this ideal grazing land and watched for signs of life. All they could see, however, was the hypnotic motion of the tall grass as it continued to roll with the wind as do the waves of the sea.

Julio Sandoval had been selected as the wagonmaster before the little band left Mesilla, and on this first night out, on this cold, November evening, Sandoval selected those whom he would use as sentries. Joaquin and Ruben were to stand watch at the northeastern points of the caravan, while Emilio and Enrique were to protect the southwestern.

After supper had been eaten and a last cup of coffee drunk, the men rolled themselves up into their warm, woolen blankets and fell asleep. A few pinon and juniper bushes spotted the San Augustin Pass and they comprised the extent of anything which could be considered concealment. The first night on the trail was a typical New Mexico winter night, calm, cold, and clear. The early evening breeze had depleted into the usual still night. The nutritious native grass now raised its head in a stiff proud fashion not unfamiliar to all living things in this wondrous land. On such a clear, quiet night, sounds of any magnitude, of any distance, could be heard as if they were only feet away. A calm, still night was the usual occurrence, not the exception for these descendents of the conquistadores. The dark skinned, brown-eyed sons of Spanish heritage stood watch as their friends and brothers, and neighbors slept by the campfires in their frontier comfort and safety.

Before the sun had a chance to peek over the high ridges of the Sacramento Mountains which loomed darkly far to the east, the sentries woke everyone to the smell of fresh coffee and the aroma of a tasty New Mexico breakfast which Manuel, the cook, had prepared for that hardy group of explorer pioneers. Julio's powerful voice sounded in the quiet darkness and his men rolled one by one from their blankets, pulling on their boots, and trudging toward the breakfast fire.

"We move out in one hour, so do not waste too much time in eating. Save some of it for gathering, watering, and yoking the oxen." As he issued orders, Sandoval walked about the camp making sure that everyone had rolled out. He munched on a tortilla as he went. "We'll make camp wherever we can tonight, and camp at Andreacito the next. So conserve all of the water you can today, for we may have a dry camp tonight." With that, he strode off to give instructions to the advance scouts.

"We chose the right wagonmaster," Orlando said with a chuckle. "If we don't succeed, it surely won't be because of Julio; he's one rare hombre." He drained the last of the coffee in his cup and took his dishes to the cook wagon saying, "I guess I'd better get my oxen."

The rest of the men followed his lead, those who hadn't finished, taking hasty gulps and throwing the dregs on the fire before going for their teams. Before the sun appeared over the Sacramentos, the column had already been on the move for some time, moving cautiously down the eastern slopes of the San Augustin Pass. Sandoval rode back along the column, warning, "The Apaches probably saw our fires last night and so we'd better be on our toes. You will not see them, but they'll see us and they'll be out there waiting and watching for us to do something stupid, so don't do anything to accommodate them!"

On the third day, the southern portion of the white sands came into view. The mile after mile of white gypsum sand dunes were so dazzling they could cause a blindness similar to snow blindness. Nothing in the world could surpass the pure whiteness of these sands. The wild creatures who lived in the sands had assumed the same white color for self protection. That night then, they were doubly grateful when they camped beside the waters of Andreacito. Never had water looked so cool and inviting.

For the remainder of their journey, the caravan skirted the outer perimeter of the sands as it edged toward the grasslands to the east. In the distance, the green which bordered the Tularosa River looked especially verdant after the glare of the sands.

"That must be where the Tularosa River reaches the flatlands with its precious water," Joaquin shouted to Ruben who was walking beside the carreta ahead of him.

"It sure looks good from here," Ruben called back over his shoulder.

When the wagon train reached the lush green of the grasslands bordering the Tularosa River, the men saw game of every description. The oxen were unyoked and led to the river to water and be turned loose, and after the horses had drunk, they began to graze contentedly as their riders stretched their legs.

"Ruben," Joaquin said to his friend, "it looks too good to be true, doesn't it?"

"Si, compadre, it does look too good to be true and it probably is," Ruben answered as his eyes scanned the area. "Remember, this is Apache country and I cannot believe that they will permit us to steal this place from them. I wonder how long it will be before they visit us?" He looked at the mountains towering over them and then his eyes searched their surrounding area, "This is going to be one night when I will sleep with one eye open and a rifle across my chest. This land is too rich for it to be relinquished without a challenge, and the Apaches will issue that challenge before too long, mark my words!"

As the would-be settlers had known, high up in the Sierra Blancas, the Apaches were aware that strangers had come to the Tularosa country and furthermore they appeared to be readying themselves to build a settlement. The Apaches were well aware of what that meant, but hoped since the men had not brought their womenfolk, perhaps that was not their intention. Whatever their intentions, the Apache scouts would soon know, for they would watch closely the activities of the men.

Crazy Legs and Great Star decided to investigate the newcomers for themselves and it was a cold, brisk morning with the silent snowflakes blanketing the ground as the two walked their horses slowly down the western slope of the Sierra Blancas. They threaded their way through giant Ponderosa pines, some of which were so huge that two men could not have joined hands around their trunks. They could see a steady stream of smoke as it rose into the still morning air from the campfires of the strangers who were camped only a few miles from the foot of the mountains. Several hours later, they dismounted and hobbled their horses and proceeded on foot to reconnoiter. They moved carefully down toward the campfires, selecting a path which provided the most cover. They reached the shelter of huge boulders around which scrub oak and other low vegetation grew in abundance, thus making this an excellent location from which to observe the movement and activity of those below them. The boulders were so large, that when Crazy Legs and Great Star stood up, they could barely see over them. The snow was not falling at this lower elevation, and the newcomers went about their tasks in an orderly fashion.

They saw one man driving an ox-drawn carreta which carried wooden barrels filled with water toward some men who had their pant legs rolled to their knees while they stomped mud with their bare feet. Two other men were cutting weeds and tall grasses and distributing these as evenly as they could beneath the feet of the stompers. The man with the cart poured water into the mixture of mud and grasses from a wooden bucket. Two other men shoveled the mud into wooden forms which measured perhaps eighteen inches long and twelve inches wide and four or five inches deep. The Apaches were witnessing the making of adobe bricks. When the mud had dried sufficiently, the forms would be removed and the bricks stacked to dry in the sun.

Crazy Legs and Great Star also observed the guards who constantly patrolled on the outer perimeter of the camp, and they watched with interest two men who were sawing boards. A large platform had been constructed of pine logs not far from the adobe makers and one man stood on top of this platform and one beneath it. The man on top pulled up on a long saw blade while the man underneath pulled down on the blade, thereby cutting boards out of large tree trunks.

The two brothers decided to spend the night at their observation post so that they could know how late into the night the strangers worked, and at what time in the morning they returned to work. They took turns sleeping and keeping watch, and before the sun rose, the men had once more begun their work, and on this day, some of them continued to build the bricks while others began to construct walls from the adobes already deemed sufficiently dry enough to do so.

Small houses were being constructed, the walls of which were about eight feet high. Peeled logs were then placed across the top of the walls about two feet apart and then small juniper limbs, as straight as possible, and a little smaller than a man's wrists, were fastened across these logs to finish the construction of the ceilings.

Close to the center of the partially constructed homes, a few men were working on what seemed to be an adobe corral. The highest part of the wall was about five feet tall and apparently the men intended for the rest of it to be no taller. There was only one gate, a heavy one constructed of boards and logs. The brothers knew that this is where the livestock would be kept at night to be turned out under guard every morning. At the end of their second day of watching, Crazy Legs and Great Star decided that they had seen enough and pulled back to return to their village.

When they were once more seated before the fire in their parents' tepee, they told them of what they had seen. "My guess," Great Star said as he leaned to place another piece of wood on the fire, "is that when these Mexicans finish building their homes, barns and corrals, and irrigation systems, they will go back to the Rio Grande to get their families. How long, I wonder, will it be before others develop villages on the eastern side of our mountain along the Hondo and Pecos Rivers?"

"They're beginning to corral us in, here on the Sierra," Crazy Legs added as he stared into the fire. "Some of our braves have already made raids on the settlement on the Tularosa, but it does not seem to deter the determination of the Mexicans to stay. They will, however, furnish our young warriors with a source of food and horses and excitement. It will be a close source and as the village grows, our raids will be more frequent and eventually the Mexicans will begin to retaliate. Then the soldiers will side with the Mexicans and the noose will tighten even more, and once a village is started on the Pecos River, the noose will be that much tighter."

"All this land was once ours," Thunderbolt said when his son had finished talking, "my grandfather and his father's people were the only ones to live here. Our enemies were the Comanches to the south and the Navajos to the north. But no one threatened to drive us from our land as the people do now. The sad thing is that we have nowhere to go, for the Americans are beginning to be everywhere."

Evening Star rose while her husband was talking and in a few minutes she returned and handed each of them a cigarette, the tobacco of which was rolled in an oak leaf. Thunderbolt took a small stick from the fire and lit his cigarette. He then held out the stick for the others to use.

"My brother," Great Star smiled as he slapped his brother's knee, "Why don't we make a trip to the Mexican village on the Tularosa and bring back a few horses from that corral of theirs, what do you say?"

"Why not?" Crazy Legs rose, "do you have a plan?"

"Of course, you're not the only one who can make a plan, you know," grinned his brother.

Thunderbolt's and Evening Star's eyes met for a second and pride and amusement could be seen in their glance.

"What you should be doing, both of you," Evening Star said

with a smile, "is looking for wives."

"Did you hear what mother said, Crazy Legs? You should be looking for a wife, not running around with your brother, looking for horses! I agree with her." Great Star wore a grin as wide as the quarter moon which hung in the sky. "I'll tell you what . . . I'll go down to the Mexican village and steal those horses while you visit the young maidens in our village. What do you say to that plan?"

Crazy Legs threw a small rock at his brother. "When I go a courting the maidens, my brother, you might as well go after Mexican horses, because you wouldn't have a chance."

"That's what I like about you," Great Star was still grinning as he walked through the flap of the tepee. "You're not the least bit modest."

"If you two great warriors wouldn't mind, why don't you let this aging warrior in on your plan," Thunderbolt joked.

Great Star re-entered, let the flap fall back into place and returned to the fire, "Why not?"

"Father, your son the strategist, is about to enlighten us in the art of raiding; shall we permit ourselves to be honored with his advice?"

Evening Star looked over her shoulder, smiled and shook her head as she continued to tidy up the tepee.

The three men grew serious now as Great Star leveled the ground in front of him with the palm of his hand. With a small stick, he drew on the ground a map of the new village. "Here," he pointed with the stick, "is the adobe corral, and here is the entrance, the only one. As we observed during our visit, all of the horses and oxen were driven into the corral at sundown, and the heavy gate closed and barred with a huge log. Two guards are posted, one at each side of the gate, to prevent anyone from opening the gate to steal the animals. What I propose to do is to steal up on the backside of corral, climb the wall and drop inside. And you, my brother, will stay on the outside of the wall."

"Oh, I see," smiled Crazy Legs, "and at that point you will hand me the horses one by one. Do you think you can lift a horse over a five foot wall?"

Great Star laughed his slow laugh and then became serious once more. "When I am in the corral, you can hand me one end of a rope which I will bring with me; we will lay it across the top of the wall and each of us will hold it tightly, using it as a saw to saw down through the wall in two places, until we have a gap wide enough and deep enough to lead out the horses. What do you think of that plan, chiefs?''

"That plan is so crazy it might work! Let's try it for real.''

The two Apaches moved carefully, slowly through the brush and sacaton toward the adobe corral. When the wall had been reached, they halted, becoming motionless as their senses searched for danger. The two guards were mumbling, but what they said was indistinguishable to the listeners. The brothers glanced at one another and then Crazy Legs made a stirrup of his hands and Great Star stepped up to the top of the wall and quietly let himself down on the other side. When he dropped into the corral, the livestock became restless and the guards stopped talking and listened, but when the animals settled down again, they began to talk quietly once more.

The sawing process began and continued, with pauses now and then to make sure the guards had not been alerted, until a fair sized gap had been created and four horses had been carefully led through the hole in the wall. Brush was then placed into the gap to prevent the other animals from attempting to escape and thus alerting the guards.

When they rode into camp and halted in front of the tepee of their parents, their parents opened the flap and stepped out. They smiled broadly when they saw their sons with the four new horses.

"See, I told you my brother was a great strategist!'' Crazy Legs smiled proudly at his brother and then turning to his parents he leaned from his horse and added, "of course he had a good teacher.''

"I heard that,'' Great Star chuckled as he slid from the back of his pony. "It has been known that some students even surpass their teachers in talent, strategy, and cunning!''

Wailing could now be heard from the far reaches of the camp and Evening Star looked in that direction and then back at her husband and sons. "Some warriors were not as lucky as you, my sons,'' she said sadly. "Seven braves followed Two Hands on a raid which took them beyond Santa Fe and only four came back. They returned shortly after you left. The dead warriors' homes and property were destroyed early this morning as is our law. After a suitable period of time, the women will remarry.''

The rays of the sun could be seen as they shone through both sides of the tepee flap for the tepees of the Apache also faced eastward and they were arranged in a row.

Evening Star was the first to rise from beneath her buffalo robe; she was the only woman of Thunderbolt for she would not have it any other way, and her husband respected her wishes. Other warriors had more than one woman and each of them had her own tepee. A warrior usually had a favorite wife, not necessarily the first one, but the one best loved. The warriors often married the widows of warriors killed in raids so that they would not be left alone, unprotected. Some warriors also had slaves, usually Mexican girls captured on a raid, to do the work for their wives.

Evening Star didn't approve of the practice and had no slaves. She had reflected many times that it might have been her Puritan heritage which accounted for her feelings. Whatever the reason, Thunderbolt honored her wishes, such was his love for his wife.

Hardly anything escaped the eyes of Thunderbolt, and when his wife slipped from under her robe, he also arose, dressed and stepped out of the tepee. He looked in the direction of the rising sun, raised his head and hands upward, toward the heavens, and closed his eyes as he began his early morning prayer to Usen.

"Oh glorious Father of the universe, giver of good health, courage, skill, and cunning, permit us, oh sacred One, to reflect your wisdom and courage here on this earth, on this day, on this sacred mountain, now. Guide us in our humble attempt to please Your understanding nature, and forgive our mistakes, for they are not done intentionally, but in ignorance of Your ways and wishes."

At the completion of his prayer, Thunderbolt lowered his arms, opened his eyes and gazed into the sky.

His wife and his two sons watched with respect from their seated positions around the fire within the tepee. They could just see his deerskin leggings and moccasins as he continued to commune with his Maker.

"What is he doing now?" Crazy Legs asked his mother.

"He's enjoying the peace and serenity of Usen's work. Do not disturb him; he will enter when he feels it is time," she replied. She busied herself in preparing breakfast.

Great Star grunted, "We Apaches live by Usen's law every minute and every day of our lives while the white man has but one day which he calls the sabbath for pleasing Usen. The rest of the days are spent disobeying Usen's laws. No wonder they believe in a place they call hell. Thank Usen that we do not have such a place or have need of one. The white man is a selfish person; he goes to his holy place of worship because he wants to make sure that he will go to the sky place, up in the clouds. His behavior after he leaves his house of worship takes on a different meaning, however. He lies, cheats, steals, and even kills, but he believes that these bad deeds will be forgiven and overlooked if he will just be present in the holy house of worship on Sunday." He shook his head, "It is amazing the extent to which people will go for self-interest."

Thunderbolt now entered the tepee and joined his sons by the fire, and said as he sat down, "Do you remember the Apache warrior our people called Wolfways? He committed the most serious crime which any Apache can do by betraying his people. For this crime, our people banished him from our tribe and country, punishment worse than death to an Apache. Well, I've heard that he and his band are committing atrocious crimes on the people around Socorro. Crimes which have caused the indignation of all of the white eyes. The dastardly acts have brought the attention of the authorities in Santa Fe and of course the army. If these outlaws are not stopped, other Apaches will be punished for their crimes. I am convinced that he is committing such horrible crimes because he is seeking revenge upon the Apaches who banished him from his tribe and family.

"Wolfways will increase his atrocities in number and cruelty until the army is sent out to punish all Apaches. Innocent Apaches would be hunted down as wild animals and be killed by the people seeking revenge against Wolfways. Meanwhile, he will sit by his campfire at night and smile at the misfortune that he has brought down upon us. He knows that most Americans do not distinguish between outlaws like himself and Apaches such as we are. He knows that to Americans, Apaches are Apaches and when one Apache kills or steals, all Apaches are guilty of the deed.

"What do you say to the three of us tracking down the evil one and putting a stop to his mischief? We could go to Fort Stanton first and inform the army of what we plan to do and why?"

"Wolfways is an evil one, all right. I remember when I caught him trying to steal one of my horses. He denied it, of course, saying the horse had left the herd and he had found it and was returning it. I think we should go after the scoundrel and put a stop to his renengade ways before any more Apaches are hurt," Crazy Legs said firmly.

"You can count on me," Great Star added.

CHAPTER FIFTEEN

T hunderbolt led his two sons down Gavilan Canyon toward Fort Stanton. As they neared the fort, they passed the small cemetery which was perhaps half a mile to the east of the fort.

The three Apaches halted at the western end of the cemetery waiting for someone to recognize them. They sat their horses side by side, their rifles cradled in their arms. In a matter of moments, a trooper could be heard calling, "Corporal of the guard, post number three!"

The corporal came running and when he saw the three motionless Apaches, he turned and yelled, "Officer of the day, post number three!"

Now the three Apaches saw an officer walking toward post number three, and upon arriving, he turned toward them. As he did so, they gave the sign of peace and called, "Nejeunee!"

The officer turned to his corporal and asked, "What did they say?"

"Friends, sir," the corporal answered. "They come as friends."

The fort had no walls around it, and on its east side the Bonito River flowed down from its source in the Sierra Blancas.

"Bring me my horse," the officer ordered the private on guard duty, "and corporal, inform Major McCarthy of what is happening here. Tell him that I will ride out to meet with these Apaches and if their presence warrants a meeting with him, I'll bring them in."

"Yes sir," the corporal replied with a snappy salute.

"This one is green, father," Crazy Legs said without making any move, without looking at his father as he spoke.

"You are right, my son, so do not do anything that could give him cause to mistrust us."

The lieutenant rode toward the Apaches at a walk, keeping his eyes fixed on the three of them. Upon reaching the Mescaleros, he raised his hand in salute and asked, "May I be of some assistance?"

Thunderbolt saw fear in the young lieutenant's eyes as he nervously shifted his weight in his stirrups.

"We come as friends, Lieutenant. We mean no harm to you or to anyone here at Fort Stanton. We would consider it an act of kindness if you would take us to Major McCarthy," Thunderbolt told him in a friendly tone of voice.

"What is your business with the major?" The lieutenant was trying, with small success, to appear calm and in command of the situation.

"Lieutenant," Thunderbolt replied patiently, "my business is with the major. It will concern you only if the major wishes it to. Relax, Lieutenant, we are friendly Apaches and we . . ." Before Thunderbolt could finish talking, he heard someone call out his name, and as he looked past the lieutenant, he saw the major cantering toward them. He turned back to the young lieutenant and said kindly, "Here is the major now."

"Welcome . . . it's good see you again," the major greeted them. He reined his horse in beside the lieutenant's mount.

"To what do I owe the pleasure of this visit? Oh, by the way, this is my adjutant, Lieutenant Wells."

The three Apaches nodded at the lieutenant. "We come to offer you our help in tracking down the renegade Apache, Wolfways. My sons and I do not want his bloodstained hands to bring down another war upon us. There has been too much killing already between our people. The killing must be stopped and if we do not put a stop to Wolfways, he and his band will bring much suffering, death, misery, and destruction to the healing process which must come between our two ways of life. All of us, your people and mine, must find a fair and just way to make the future one of harmony and understanding between our peoples."

"I agree with your thinking," the major returned, "and I welcome your aid in locating Wolfways. Indeed, he must be stopped before hatred against the Apache explodes.

"Lieutenant, prepare sleeping quarters for our guests and then report to me for dinner. I want you to get acquainted with my friends."

"Yes sir," the lieutenant replied. He gave the major a salute and rode back toward the fort at a brisk trot.

The major turned back toward the three Apaches and said, "He is new here at the fort and he's as green as they make them at West Point, but I think he has the makings of a good officer. He does not dislike your people as some officers do. I do not think that I have any officers under my command who do dislike your people. That should make things easier for both of our peoples, in this part of the country at least, to learn to live together with respect, if not amicably. You know, Thunderbolt, that we have our Wolfways also, but I'm sure your're aware of that. Let's hope that we can minimize these people's influence on the higher authorities, some of whom I'm sure you also know do not like any Indians. I'm afraid that we have our work cut out for us, my friend, and I'm sure there will be many reverses before we find a peaceful and durable way to live side by side. But what is the alternative? That would be much worse. Let's go to my quarters and continue our discussion there. It isn't very polite of me to sit here without inviting you to the fort. We've made some improvement since the fire!"

"We Apaches are accustomed to meeting out of doors, so don't apologise," Thunderbolt answered.

After dinner, the three Apaches and the major and the lieutenant sat down in the major's living room to make plans for the capture of Wolfways.

"We know of at least four ranches around the Socorro area which have been burnt out, with the loss of all of the people on those ranches. We do not know if he is still in that area or has left it," the major told them as he offered each of them a cigar.

"How many days has it been since Wolfways burnt out the last ranch?" inquired Thunderbolt.

"Three days," the major replied as he blew smoke toward the ceiling.

"Do you know, by any chance, in what area he was raiding before he went to Socorro?" Crazy Legs asked.

"Over Silver City way, I think . . . why?" asked the major.

"How many targets did he hit in that area?"

"Let me think a minute," the major said. He closed his eyes, bowed his head and rubbed his forehead with his hand. "I'm not sure . . . what difference does it make, anyway?" He looked up at Thunderbolt.

"It might make a lot of difference, Major, please try to remember," Crazy Legs told him.

"It was four," the lieutenant interrupted, "I saw the report also."

"How may days elapsed between the last raid near Silver City and the first raid in the Socorro area?" Crazy Legs leaned forward.

"If my memory serves me correctly, it was four days," the major replied.

The three Apaches glanced at one another and then Thunderbolt looked at the major and said, "It's a good chance that Wolfways will strike again tomorrow, but I don't know where. Four is a sacred number with the Apaches, and it is my guess that he is hoping that Usen will protect him if he stays with the four day pattern. When he does strike, you can be certain that he will hit four targets in the same area."

"I guess the only thing we can do, then, is to wait to see where

Wolfways strikes next and when he does strike, we move out in force. Do you agree, Thunderbolt?" the major asked.

"We can make our preparations tonight to be ready to move out as soon as we hear where Wolfways is. In that way, we may prevent him from striking at a second target. Won't the wireless inform you when and where he strikes?" Thunderbolt asked.

"Lieutenant, go over to the telegraph office and tell the sergeant to report to me immediately, day or night, no matter what the hour, when any report comes in of an Apache raid," Major Mc-Carthy ordered.

"Yes sir," the lieutenant rose, saluted, and left the room.

"Major," Thunderbolt had an interested expression on his face, "would you mind telling us a little bit about the telegraph? I know that you've had it for some years, but I never did know much about it, except that a message can travel over the wires somehow."

The major smiled as he leaned forward in his chair. "The telegraph was invented in 1844 by a man named Samuel Morse. It wasn't introduced out here in the West until a few years ago. It has a little gadget which sends messages by a code of dots and dashes over wires which also carry an electric current. The first message which Morse sent said, 'What Hath God Wrought'. It was carried over the electric wire for a short distance of only forty miles. After he successfully proved his invention all kinds of people wanted to get in on this good deal and too many people were sending messages at the same time over the same wire and it became confusing as you can well imagine. So all of these people did a smart thing. They all got together and formed a company which they called Western Union.

"If Wolfways strikes again, we should hear about it very quickly. I'll assign Lieutenant Wells to stand by with a contingent of sixteen experienced men and once we receive word of Wolfways' latest attack, we will rush to the area and you and your sons will accompany him as scouts and advisors and assist him in any way that will result in the death or capture of Wolfways. Do you agree with my plan, Thunderbolt?"

"It's a starting point," answered Thunderbolt, "but we will need the latitude to use our best judgment and strategy to put in place whatever plan will be needed at a given time and place to bring about the capture of Wolfways."

"That sounds fair enough to me. My instructions to Lieutenant Wells will encompass all that you have just conveyed to me.

Now tell me what you will need and I will see that you have it," the major told him.

"We'll need rations and ammunition for a least a couple of weeks," Thunderbolt said, "and I'd like uniforms for myself and two sons, and all of your men to have with them a complete change of clothes, Apache clothing."

"Apache clothing?" The major was surprised, "Why in heaven's name do my men need Apache clothing?" He smiled as he stopped talking, "I shouldn't have asked the question . . . I know you have your reasons and it will be as you say."

"Thank you, major, for your trust and for your faith in my sons and me. And I also want to thank you for the pleasant evening. I think my sons and I will turn in now, for we may have to leave early in the morning."

It was nearly eleven o'clock the next morning, however, before Sergeant O'Roark rushed out of the telegraph office and ran toward that of Major McCarthy. Within minutes of his arrival, the bugle call to boots and saddles was sounded by Private Lancaster who stood at attention on the porch of the major's office. Lieutenant Wells ran from his quarters, fastening his sidearms around his waist as he ran down the steps. "Sergeant McGee, assemble the men immediately. We move out in ten minutes."

"Yes sir!" Sergeant McGee's loud, authoritative voice was heard over the call of the bugle and the rustling of horses and men as they scrambled to form ranks. Major McCarthy stepped out of his office and onto the porch as Lieutenant Wells yelled, "Attention!"

The major returned his salute and shouted, "As you were men. You men were placed on full alert last night because we were expecting an attack on civilians in this area by the Apache renegade, Wolfways. Well, he has struck at the Grinnel Ranch, east of Gallinas Peak. I have just received confirmation of the dastardly act of butchery. Lieutenant Wells?"

"Yes sir?"

"Bring this butcher back to me dead or alive . . . and I don't care which. Now move out."

"In columns of two," the lieutenant ordered, "Hoooo!"

The three Apaches had already ridden out of the fort as the column moved out, led by Lieutenant Wells with Sergeant McGee at his side. They loped their horses past the stables and down the gradual slope toward the Bonito River, and within a few minutes all that could be seen of the passing of the troopers was the cloud of dust which was blowing gently eastward.

The troopers made a swing toward the northwest after they splashed through the shallow waters of the Bonito. A few miles further on they would head due north, skirting the western end of the mountain range called La Sierra. It was a straight shot of relatively open and rolling country to the village of Gallinas which was located not far from Gallinas Peak. Lieutenant Wells hadn't seen Thunderbolt or his sons since he had left Fort Stanton, but as he led his men northward, he saw them sitting their motionless horses perhaps half a mile ahead. When the column reached the Apaches, he halted his command and gave them a break while he talked with the Apache scouts.

"There is a mining camp on the southeastern end of Gallinas Peak, and my sons and I, as well as most Apaches, know that the mine's supply wagons arrive at the camp once a month. The supply train could be a target for Wolfways, but we have no way to be certain that this will be his next target. It is only a possibility. Another such possibility, however, could be the Burgerin Ranch, near Ancho. I believe that this ranch would be a good target, simply because it is isolated and does not have much manpower. Still another possible target would be the Chavez Ranch, near Duran. We do not believe that Wolfways would be foolish enough to chance a raid on the gold mining town of White Oaks in the Jicarilla Mountains. The places I have just mentioned are from thirty to fifty miles from where Wolfways last struck. It seems very likely to me that one of the three I've told you about will be the next target. With the one he has already struck, those three would total the Apache sacred number, four. After he has ravaged these places, he will move on to a new location and begin his carnage all over again. What we have to decide is which target he will hit next, and intercept him before he strikes," Thunderbolt concluded.

"Is it possible that he will strike at some target other than the ones which you've suggested?" the lieutenant asked.

"We do not think so, lieutenant, he seems to strike places in one general area before moving on. Judging his past performance, these three seem to meet his requirements best," Thunderbolt replied.

"I see," replied the young officer. He sat silently for a few seconds, then "What do you suggest, Thunderbolt?"

"It would seem like a wise idea to me if you and most of your men would station themselves as nearly as possible in the center of these three potential targets. That location would be at Gallo

Arroyo. Once we've located Wolfways and his band, you can make your move from there," the scout told him.

"How do you propose to locate him?"

"By having two of your men dress as Apaches and accompany me as I search the area around Duran. If we spot him, I'll send one of your men to inform you. You will send two men with Crazy Legs and they will scout the area around Ancho. The third party, under Great Star will scout the area for the wagon train."

"Why do my men have to dress as Apaches?"

"If you were Wolfways and saw soldiers, what would you do?"

"I see what you mean," the lieutenant answered sheepishly.

"But if he saw other Apaches in the area, he would either ask for their help or figure that he had not been discovered by the white people yet, and so he still has time to conduct his next raid," Thunderbolt explained.

"How will you find us at Gallo Arroyo? That arroyo is many miles long," the lieutenant pointed out.

"There is a thirty foot drop in the arroyo over a stone ledge which is a waterfall when the water is running. The arroyo should be dry at this time of year. Wait there until one of us comes for you," Thunderbolt said. "When one of us does come for you, I want you to send two of your men for the other two parties. When this happens, you know what to do. You will have with you ten men plus the three scouts. When you reach the target, hide yourselves well, so that Wolfways will not suspect that you are there. When the rest of us reach the location, we will scatter ourselves in the surrounding area behind the renegades.

"When the attack begins, you should be able to kill a few of the warriors with your surprise firepower; the warriors will be confused by what they have run up against, and may retreat. At that point we will strike, hoping to kill or capture Wolfways. If we succeed in killing or capturing him, the rest of the band will disperse and we hope we'll never hear of or see them again. It is my guess, and this is only a guess, that Wolfways and his braves are hiding out near Pinos Wells. It would be a good spot to wait for the right time to attack the Chavez Ranch. It has plenty of water for his men and horses, and food, for the deer, antelope, and other wild life water there. The country is broken up enough to supply plenty of shelter for their concealment."

"It seems that your thinking is without flaw, Thunderbolt, I cannot improve upon it, so why don't we implement your plan?"

Once more they rode northward, and several hours later, they split up into the four different parties.

Meanwhile, Wolfways and his warriors were approaching Pinos Wells. "We will water here and then make camp in the deep arroyo just north of the waterhole," he told his men.

As they dismounted, their horses walked to the edge of the water and began to drink. The warriors went to some distance and threw small rocks into the water, making ripples, and then they, too, drank. The ripples prevented their seeing themselves in the water, which was against Usen's law.

"We will wait in the big arroyo until the fourth day since our attack on the Grinnel Ranch. This will give the people in the area sufficient time to decide we've moved on. They will not expect our attack on the Chavez Ranch and therefore will be unprepared."

Thunderbolt stopped with the two Apache clad soldiers about ten miles south of Pinos Wells. "I will station myself on top of this hill where you'll be able to see me. I want you, Gillis, to ride directly east at a trot for thirty minutes, watching for hoofprints which could have been made by Wolfways and his warriors. At the end of the thirty minutes, look for the top of this hill, and as best you can, using the top of the hill as the central point, move in a circular pattern, turning north first. You, Mills, will ride west, doing the same thing. Only when you have ridden the thirty minutes, turn south. The two of you should reach the starting point of each other's circle in about two hours or so. The straight riding line of the thirty minute ride should disclose any hoofprints, but if either of you should miss them, the circular ride will give you a second chance to pick them up. At your thirty minute location, each of you pile some rocks in a place where it will be easy for the other to see them. If you should see tracks before you complete your ride, report back here to me. I will then signal with this broken piece of mirror for the others to come in. If you see my signal, please answer with your mirror. If you have no questions or suggestions, move out."

Thunderbolt tied his horse to a juniper limb and walked to a clearing at the top of the knoll. His eyes searched the open country which lay on all sides of him, looking for sign. When none could be seen, he turned to watch Gillis as he trotted toward the east bending to look for tracks. He finally disappeared behind some of the scrub juniper and cedar which dotted the open country. Thunderbolt then turned to watch Mills as he also rode out, watching him as he grew smaller in the distance. Because the terrain was more open, he could watch him as he reached the open, grassy prairie. He knew that it would be more difficult for Mills to locate tracks because of the thickly growing grass. Suddenly, Mills stopped and looked to his left and then quickly to his right. He then dismounted and knelt on one knee to inspect the ground more closely. After a few moments of inspection, Thunderbolt saw him stand once more to look to his right. Within a few minutes, Mills climbed into his saddle and reined his horse to return in the direction he had left, his heels flapping against the belly of his horse, giving the appearance of a bird flapping its wings as it took flight.

"He's found Wolfway's trail," Thunderbolt said.

When Mills rode up to where Thunderbolt waited, he said as he swung from his saddle, "I've found his trail and it looked like he was heading for Pinos Wells. The tall grass over which they rode was bent in the direction of the Wells, and some of it was even broken off. The hoofprints showed that they were not shod ponies. I'm not too good at this, but I'd guess he had between five and ten men with him."

"Good work, Mills." Thunderbolt turned to face the direction in which Gillis had ridden. He took out his mirror and tilted it so that the sun's rays were reflected in it. After his third attempt, Gillis repeated the signal, and within a short time he could be seen racing his horse in their direction as his horse dodged the low, scrubby trees.

"Mills, ride to Gallo Arroyo and tell the lieutenant that I believe that Wolfways' next target will be the Chavez Ranch."

He watched as Mills once more rode off at a trot. It would be a good three hour ride or better from the Wells to the headquarters of the Chavez Ranch, thought Thunderbolt. When Gillis had neared the bottom of the hill, Thunderbolt untied his horse, pulled himself into the saddle, and rode to meet him.

"Let's ride till we find a good place to camp for the night, Gillis, and at sunup we'll ride to the Chavez Ranch and find my sons and the men with them."

By midday, Thunderbolt and Gillis had secluded themselves among some huge boulders, juniper trees and small cedars about two miles from the Chavez headquarters, where they kept watch for any sign of Thunderbolt's sons and the men with them.

"There," Gillis finally said. He pointed to three riders off at some distance. "Would that be some of our men? There are three of them."

"Yes, it's Crazy Legs," Thunderbolt answered slowly as his eyes followed the riders, "ride out and bring them back here, Gillis."

While Gillis rode to meet Crazy Legs, Thunderbolt saw three more riders far to the south. "Probably Great Star," he swung into the saddle and rode out of his hiding place, galloping toward the three riders. Thirty minutes later, the three different groups had met, decided upon their plan of attack and ridden out to prepare for it.

Vicente Chavez had concealed some of Lieutenant Wells' troopers in his barn, some in his house, and some behind his stone corrals. He and his family busied themselves with the usual chores, none of them too far from cover. They tried as best they could to give the appearance that they suspected nothing. It was around noon on the fourth day, when Lieutenant Wells whispered from the window, "Get your family into the house, Vicente, the Apaches have been spotted."

Vicente and his sons, aged twelve and fourteen, were the only ones outside the house when the lieutenant alerted them. His wife and daughter, aged eighteen, were busily preparing the noon meal. It appeared that Wolfways had chosen meal time to strike, for this way the family would be in one building and in one room, and there would be little chance of their spotting his men when they crept up to surround the house.

"That scroungy, murdering, sorry no good so-and-so," the lieutenant muttered, "he doesn't overlook a single detail. If we were not here, the Chavez family would be caught completely by surprise as they ate and would be shot down without being able to fire one shot in their defense."

Mrs. Chavez and her daughter, Amelia, stayed clear of the windows, but readied themselves to lend assistance, wherever and whenever they were needed. Vicente and his two sons, Eli and Eloy crouched by a window, with rifles in their hands.

"Are they near the house yet?" Vicente whispered to the lieutenant.

"We only saw one for a split second as he dashed from one location to another. It won't be long, now, though, so be ready."

"They're close, lieutenant; I can smell them," Sergeant

McGee whispered. He checked his rifle one more time.

A shot rang out and then another, and then a third, as an Apache slid by the window and lay dead on the porch.

"How did he get to the house without being spotted?" the lieutenant whispered to his sergeant.

"Welcome to the world of the Apache, sir," the sergeant peered out of his window. "I'll bet they'll rush the house in a minute . . ." He had no time to finish his sentence as gunfire was heard from the direction of the barn and corrals. At the same instant, another Apache rushed the door, rifle in hand and with yellow warpaint in stripes under his eyes.

Eloy was the first to fire and his brother Eli shot almost simultaneously, hitting the warrior and bringing him down.

All then became nervously quiet, for what seemed a long period of time until suddenly another shot was heard from the vicinity of Crazy Legs, Great Star, and Thunderbolt, and then two more shots rang out.

It was quiet again, too quiet, and Lieutenant Wells called out, "Thunderbolt, are you out there?"

Horses could be heard now as the people inside the house saw three Apaches racing westward toward the Indian ruins of Gran Quivera. Lieutenant Wells stepped out onto the porch of the ranchhouse and yelled again, "Where are you, Thunderbolt?"

"We are over here," came the voice of Great Star.

Lieutenant Wells looked in the direction of the voice and saw his soldiers, still dressed in their Apache clothing, walking slowly toward him, but Crazy Legs and Great Star remained behind.

"What happened back there?"

"It's Thunderbolt," one of his men answered, "he tried to take Wolfways alive, but I guess Wolfways was determined not to be taken. Thunderbolt had a bead on him and told Wolfways to drop his rifle, which he did. Thunderbolt then stood up and walked toward Wolfways and then suddenly one of the other Apaches fired from concealment. His bullet hit Thunderbolt. Within seconds, Wolfways picked up his rifle and also fired at Thunderbolt. The second bullet finished the scout, but not before he got off a round which hit Wolfways in the chest. They're both dead."

The Apache death chant could be heard as Lieutenant Wells lowered his rifle, bowed his head and said, "Damn!"

Some time later, a single shot rang out and the soldiers raised their rifles to defend themselves.

"There's no need for that," Sergeant McGee told them as he

looked in the direction from which they'd heard the shot. "Crazy Legs and Great Star have just shot their father's horse. The Apaches believe that it takes four days of travel to reach O'zho, and to make those days of travel easier, his horse is killed so that he may ride to O'zho. As a rule the dead Apache is dressed in his finest clothing, and his weapons are also buried whth him. They believe that the way the Apache looks when he is buried is how he will look in O'zho. In their interpretation of heaven, it will look just like here on earth and there will be plenty of buffalo and deer and elk to hunt. That is why he will need his horse and weapons. Thunderbolt is a hero to the Apaches, now, because he gave his life for them." The sergeant looked out over the open country. "Thunderbolt will never ride again over the country he loved so much. He now belongs to our memories. He also died for all of us, you know, not just for his people, but the ironic thing is that the white people will not believe this. To them, he was just a dirty Apache who killed and looted. Someday, maybe all of us will come to realize that Thunderbolt was one of the first Apache Americans. He and his sons believe that the Apache way as they knew it is coming to an end and they were determined to help bridge the chasm that separates our two cultures.

"Much suffering lies ahead for the Apaches, I'm afraid, before we Americans try to understand and respect their ways and give them a hand in making that change easier. Some day we will look back in shame for not having extended our hands in friendship and help.

"Lieutenant, the Apaches never speak the name of their dead after they are buried because if they do, the ghost of the dead person will come to the caller. This may not please the ghost because he may be on a hunt or doing something else and he will not want to be interrupted. Thunderbolt's name will be used from this day forward only if his advice is badly needed."

"What about Wolfways?" the lieutenant asked.

"He was an evil man, and the Apaches believe he will be reborn as a bear and if he is a good bear, he'll enter O'zho when he is killed or dies. That is why Apaches will kill bears only in self defense. They never eat the flesh of a bear or use his fur, and they never touch a dead bear."

Lieutenant Wells made preparations to leave and Vicente Chavez and his family thanked him repeatedly for having saved their lives. The soldiers didn't move out, however, until Crazy Legs and Great Star rode out and fell into the head of the column.

The two brothers showed no emotion, which was the Apache way. Never did the Apache complain of the cold, the heat, hunger, or of any suffering they might encounter. Their pain was always locked up within them, and that was the case this day.

Lieutenant Wells and the other soldiers showed their respect for the two Apaches by riding in silence behind them. That night as the troop made camp, Crazy Legs and Great Star stayed off to themselves. After the meal was over, one of the troopers who had ridden with Thunderbolt at the fight with Wolfways, took out his harmonica and began softly, "Old Folks at Home." Crazy Legs and Great Star had never heard the tune before, but somehow they both knew the trooper was showing his respect for their father and sorrow at his death. When the trooper began to play, the two Apaches turned their heads slowly to look at the trooper. As he played, his eyes turned toward the two warriors, and Great Star and Crazy Legs each gave a small nod of acknowledgment to the trooper, who nodded in return.

A few miles before they would reach Fort Stanton, Crazy Legs and Great Star pulled away from the column and trotted their horses toward the mouth of a wide canyon. The soldiers watched their departure, but neither the Apaches nor the troopers revealed their sadness. The lieutenant turned in his saddle as he saw the Apaches trot homeward, and he nodded to his bugler. Notes of a short call, composed by the bugler at last night's camp could be heard wafting through the still air. The troopers became rigid in their saddles upon hearing the bugler's call. They stared straight ahead as they restrained their mounts who were eager for the hay and oats and rest which they knew lay not far ahead. But the soldiers who rode them appeared as wooden, so still did they sit. This unprecedented action lasted for four times four seconds, just long enough to honor the Apache sacred number.

Upon hearing the bugle's clear notes, the two brothers wheeled their ponies and sat side by side listening and watching. When it was finished, they each gave a salute and once more turned to ride up the canyon.

They had ridden only a few miles when their mother, Evening Star stepped out from the shelter of thickly growing juniper trees. "Where is your father?" But she knew the answer before her sons replied.

"He has his daughter with him, then," Evening Star spoke as she stood erect facing her sons. "Smallpox hit our village after you left, taking its toll and among the dead was your sister and her husband. Our village is no more for ashes have replaced our homes and belongings. Fire, we have learned, is the only cure for this disease. Those who survived thought it best to move to the Sierra Madres in Mexico. They wanted to put as much distance between themselves and the disease as possible; in fact they looked upon the disease as a sign that they should go. I could not leave without you, and I dared not enter Fort Stanton knowing I might carry the disease.''

Great Star spoke, ''How long have you waited, mother?'' He sat his pony stiffly.

''Two nights and two days,'' she answered.

''Let's move up the canyon a few more miles and make camp,'' Crazy Legs suggested. ''We have a lot of talking and planning to do. Great Star, find something to eat.''

Great Star checked his rifle and reined his pony away from his mother and brother and rode on ahead. He knew that wild game abounded in this deep canyon, and in a few minutes he jumped a flock of wild turkeys and brought down a fat young hen.

The three sat by their small campfire, eating their food in silence, until Evening Star spoke, ''Would you like to try the white man's ranching?''

Her two sons stopped chewing their turkey, looked at each other and then back at their mother. ''Ranching?'' they both asked simultaneously.

''Why not?'' She took another bite of the turkey. ''It's either that or being run down and being locked up on this reservation which all men are talking about. Do you want to be locked up like animals for the rest of your lives?''

''You know the answer to that,'' Great Star told her somberly. He glanced at his brother as he spoke.

''We do not have any choice,'' his mother continued, ''if we join another band of Apaches, it will only be a matter of time before the soldiers round us up and put us on a reservation. Things are moving very rapidly . . . the big war which the white man is fighting is about over, and that means that a flood of Confederates may choose to move out of the South toward the West, thereby leaving behind the bitterness and hardship which the Union may try to impose on them. When that happens, the Apache way of life will end. Why don't we homestead a choice piece of land and begin, or I should say, you begin your lives all over again? You are young, with your lives before you.''

''They won't let us Apaches homestead land, mother, you

know that," Crazy Legs told her.

"With Major McCarthy's help, perhaps we can. He surely knows someone who knows someone else who will know how we can go about getting some land," Evening Star said as she looked at her sons.

"It is worth a try," Great Star said, "what do you think, my brother?"

"If a change is to come in our lifetime, now is the time for that change. We are alone and without a home. I agree with you, mother, that we should approach Major McCarthy to see if he knows how we might be able to get a homestead," Crazy Legs decided.

When enough time had passed so that they knew Evening Star would no longer be a danger to the fort as a carrier of smallpox, the three rode down the canyon and over to Fort Stanton. Evening Star was flanked by her two sons as they dismounted in front of the major's office. The major invited them in cordially, and thoroughly approved of their decision to begin over, if possible. Accordingly, he immediately contacted the legal authorities at Fort Union, who in turn told the major that there would be no problem because Evening Star was a citizen of the United States. She would, however, have to again resume her name, Kathleen Conners, the name she had been given at birth. Otherwise, she would have to apply for citizenship before being eligible to homestead. Her two sons were automatically citizens because their mother was.

The homestead site which the Conners selected was located in the Hondo Valley, about forty miles east of the Sierra Blancas. From the highest part of the ranch which extended into the foothills, the Conners could see the snowcapped peaks of their mountain. From late October until May, this peak was covered with the snow whose precious runoff in early spring made the hidden Hondo Valley bloom into a luscious, green valley whose beauty was unsurpassed anywhere in the New Mexico Territory. The Conners' Ranch became known as the Friendship Ranch by Anglo, Mexican, and Apache travelers.

One day after they had been on the ranch for several months, Great Star was yearning for a sight of their Sacred Mountain. He asked his brother if he would like to saddle up and ride higher on the ranch where they could get a glimpse of their beloved

157

mountain in the afternoon sun.

As the two men rode away from the headquarters, Crazy Legs asked, "Is something bothering you, Great Star?"

"No," answered his brother, "I just thought you might like to ride with me to see the mountain. Usen has laid such a pretty blanket of snow on the peaks and I needed to look at it."

"You read my thoughts, Great Star; I was about to ask you the same thing."

The two men rode in silence as each remembered the good times the past had blessed them with and each thought of their father. Finally they had climbed to a spot where, through a gap in the gently rolling hills, they could see their mountain. They reined in their horses and gazed at the shining snowcovered peaks of Sierra Blanca.

Neither said anything for long moments, and then Great Star broke the silence, "Maybe Magdalena was right, maybe this is the beginning of something new, something wonderful for both America and her children of many races, colors, and religions."

"Her dream may come true," Crazy Legs leaned on his saddle horn and turned to his brother wonderingly, "when she told us of her dream, I thought some evil spirit had possessed her, but it may have been that of a good spirit, a message of hope and unity and understanding. The spirit may believe that the time has come for a new country to be born with God's blessing and guidance. One which is indivisible and which embraces liberty, equality, and justice."

"Sounds good, doesn't it?" Great Star said.

"Sounds like Magdalena's dream," Crazy Legs replied as he reined his horse in the direction of the ranch house, "let's go home, Great Star."

BIBLIOGRAPHY

Ball, Eve with Nora Henn and Lynda Sanchez. *An Apache Odyssey-Indeh*, Provo, Utah: Brigham Young University, 1980.

Barrett, S.M. *Geronimo's Story of His Life*. New York: Duffield & Company, 1906.

Cleland, Robert Glass. *This Reckless Breed of Men*. Albuquerque: University of New Mexico Press, 1950.

Cremony, John C. *Among the Apaches*. Tucson, Arizona: Arizona Silhouettes, 1951.

Driver, Harold E. *Indians of North America*. Chicago: University of Chicago Press, 1961.

Garbarino, Merwyn S. *American Indians*. Chicago: World Book Encyclopedia, 1971.

Haflen, Leroy R. and Carl Coke Rister. *Western America*. Englewood Cliffs, New Jersey: Prentice-Hall, 1941.

Herring, Hubert. *A History of Latin America*. New York: Alfred A. Knopf, 1961.

Horn, Calvin. *New Mexico's Troubled Years*. Albuquerque: Horn & Wallace, 1963.

Johnson, William Weber. *Mexico*. New York: Time Incorporated, 1961.

Keleher, William A. *The Fabulous Frontier*. Albuquerque: University of New Mexico Press, 1962.

La Farge, Oliver. *A Pictorial History of the American Indian*. New York: Crown Publishers, Inc., 1956.

Riegel, Robert E. *America Moves West*. New York: Henry Holt & Co., 1930.

Santee, Ross. *Apache Land*. Lincoln: University of Nebraska Press, 1972.

Sonnichsen, C.S. *Tularosa*. Old Greenwich, Connecticut: Devin-Adair Co., 1972.

Spence, Clark. *The American West*. New York: Crowell, 1966.

Terrell, John Upton. Apache Chronicle. *New York: World Publishing Co., 1874.*

Thrapp, Dan S. *Conquest of Apacheria*. Norman, Oklahoma: University of Oklahoma Press, 1961.

Underhill, Ruth M. *Red Man's America*. Chicago: University of Chicago Press, 1953.

Von Hagen, Victor W. *The Aztec Man and Tribe*. Vol II. New York: The Americana Corporation, 1957.